M000033241

Murder on Tap

Maple Syrup Mysteries Book 4

Emily James

Stronghold Books
ONTARIO, CANADA

Copyright © 2017 by Emily James.

All rights reserved. No part of this publication may be reproduced, distributed, or transmitted in any form or by any means, including photocopying, recording, or other electronic or mechanical methods, without the prior written permission of the author. It's okay to quote a small section for a review or in a school paper. To put this in plain language, this means you can't copy my work and profit from it as if it were your own. When you copy someone's work, it's stealing. No one likes a thief, so don't do it. Pirates are not nearly as cool in real life as they are in fiction.

For permission requests, write to the author at the address below.

Emily James
authoremilyjames@gmail.com
www.authoremilyjames.com

This is a work of fiction. I made it up. You are not in my book. I probably don't even know you. If you're confused about the difference between real life and fiction, you might want to call a counselor rather than a lawyer because names, characters, places, and incidents in this book are a product of my twisted imagination. Real locales and public names are sometimes used for atmospheric purposes. Any resemblance to actual people, living or dead, or to businesses, companies, events, and institutions is completely coincidental.

Book Layout ©2013 BookDesignTemplates
Cover Design by Deranged Doctor Designs

Murder on Tap/Emily James. -- 1st ed.
ISBN 978-1-988480-05-3

For my readers. Your encouragement and excitement make these stories an adventure to be shared. Without you, I'd be some weird lady who spends all day with her imaginary friends.

A lie may take care of the present, but it has no future.

−AUTHOR UNKNOWN

Chapter 1

From thirty feet away, I couldn't tell if Drew Harris was carving his initials into one of my trees or emptying his bladder on it. I never would have admitted it, but I was hoping for the latter. My sugar maples took forty years to mature before we could tap them for syrup. The thought of him needlessly vandalizing one made my stomach clench.

Despite what it looked like, I doubted Drew would damage one of my trees. I'd hired him to photograph Sugarwood so we'd be able to spruce up our website and create fresh promotional material. So far, Drew had shown himself to be not only talented but also professional, despite looking young enough to be barely able to vote. Or shave.

His girlfriend-assistant was another matter. She was the reason I'd left the rest of the people on the tour I was leading so that I could follow Drew out into the woods alone. Yesterday, in the sugar shack, she would have burned her hand in a vat of boiling sap, trying to taste it, if Stacey, my mechanic, hadn't stopped her. Today, the girl decided to try to juggle snowballs and accidentally smacked one of my horses in the face with one, spooking him. He'd narrowly avoided trampling a paying guest.

It had to stop. All the pictures in the world wouldn't matter if his girlfriend hurt herself or some-one else and they sued me.

But before I could find a way to gently suggest he leave her at home next time, I had to figure out a way to get him to turn around without catching a look at any part of his anatomy I didn't want to see.

I tightened my scarf around my neck and cleared my throat. "Drew?"

He held up a finger and stayed facing away from me.

Uncomfortable heat crept up the back of my neck, and I backed up a step. Really, there were certain times a person shouldn't be interrupted. My request could wait.

Drew squatted down. With the new angle, I could see that his hands were busy with his camera rather than his...something else.

He rose to his feet and turned to me, a grin on his face. "It took me a bit to figure out the best angle for the lighting." He waved me over and held up his camera. "But you're going to love this."

The image on the screen was of a knot shaped like a heart, the light gray-brown bark curling around it perfectly to make it look like it'd been stamped deeply into the tree.

It'd be ideal for mugs or postcards or advertising a special Valentine's event or sale on maple products.

A weight settled in my chest. He was one of the best photographers I'd ever seen. If I asked him not to bring his girlfriend, or assistant, or whatever she was, around anymore, he might very well quit. Especially if she was his girlfriend. No sane man would risk making a woman he loved angry at him just to keep a job. I wasn't paying him well enough for that.

And he had to love her, or he wouldn't keep bringing her along with him. She didn't even know enough about photography to be able to switch out the SD card in his camera when he needed a new one yesterday.

Maybe I could simply keep a closer watch on her rather than risk losing him as a photographer. Did they make those arm-band leashes for adults?

He clicked away from the image. "If you don't like it, I can focus on a different kind of shot."

His voice had the same awkward wounded tone to it that I used to hear in my best friend Ahanti's voice when one of her clients didn't like the tattoo she'd designed for them.

He must have misinterpreted my expression as disappointment with the image. "I do love it. I'm—"

"Riley?" The woman's voice carried through the trees from the direction of the sleigh and horses where we'd left the rest of the tour group. It had a panicky edge to it.

I spun away from Drew and jogged back toward the clearing. Next season, we were hiring a new tour guide. Wrangling guests was like herding cats. I wasn't cut out for it. This was more stressful than speaking in front of a jury.

I burst into the clearing where I'd stopped the sleigh. It was a scheduled stop in a clearing set up to show how sap collection techniques had changed over the years from wooden buckets and spouts carved by hand to the plastic tubing system we currently used.

At first glance, everything looked okay. The horses hadn't trampled anyone, and Drew's girlfriend sat in the sleigh, leaning left and right with her phone held in the air with one white-and-blue gloved hand like she was at a concert. I might have laughed at the sight if I wasn't so grateful the spotty signal was keeping her out of trouble.

I took a head count of the other eight people on the tour. The man who came with his teenage daughter and the couple in their sixties stood on the far side of the clearing as if they'd been reading the laminated historical tidbits on the display trees. All good there.

But the couple with two kids stood off to one side, closer to the horses, the dad holding their two-year-old boy in his arms and the mom turning in circles.

"Riley?" she called again, louder this time.

Their five-year-old daughter wasn't with them.

Crap! The late March weather had warmed up compared to January and early February, but not enough that a child could be lost in the woods overnight without hypothermia.

My stomach coiled into a Slinky loop. *Don't panic, Nicole. You're the one in charge.*

The mother must have spotted me because she bee-lined for me, her hands outstretched like she thought I might have a secret potion to make her daughter appear. "We were petting the horses, and when we turned around, she was gone."

My mom used to say that you could calm a frantic client by using their name. It helped establish trust. I search my memory for the woman's name. We weren't too far apart in age, and we'd chatted for a few minutes before the tour started while waiting for the rest of the registrants. She'd been telling me that this was their first time touring Sugarwood with the kids. Her husband had booked the tour that morning from work and called her as a surprise, saying Riley was finally old enough to appreciate the sleigh ride.

"Don't worry, Kristen." I squeezed one of the hands she held out to me. "She can't be far. We'll split up and look for her. If someone doesn't find her in five minutes, I'll call in help. Okay?"

My voice didn't give away how close to throwing up I felt. I split everyone up and sent them off in a starburst pattern, with instructions to walk in a straight line for five minutes and then follow their footprints back. The last thing I needed was for another person to get lost in the woods.

The older man hung back as the others set off. He was only a few inches taller than I was, and the wind had blown his thinning hair up so that the top of his head made me think of a hedgehog curling into a ball. I wouldn't have minded curling up into a ball myself right about now.

"We want to help find the little girl," he said, "but I can't leave my wife."

His hands were jammed hard in his pockets and his shoulders hunched. He didn't look back in his wife's direction, but she was watching us, so it was a safe bet she knew what he was talking to me about. She had her purple scarf wrapped around her head, protecting her ears like she was ready to trudge out into the woods.

Perhaps this was a health thing. When my grandfather developed diabetes, he'd also ended up with diabetic neuropathy, where he didn't have complete feeling in his feet. It caused him to stumble. He hadn't felt comfortable walking anywhere alone after that. If one of them had a similar medical condition, they didn't need to feel like they had to explain their private business to me.

And I certainly wasn't going to order them to split up if they felt uncomfortable doing it. This tour was already turning out to be a liability waiting to happen.

"No problem," I said. "There are enough of us that we're almost overlapping anyway. You two can stick together."

He left with a nod, and I hustled off in the direction assigned to me. Off in the distance, I could already hear others from the group calling out Riley's name. I called out as well and kept my gaze on the ground, watching for anything that could be a footprint.

The calls of the others faded slightly, and the coil in my stomach tightened. If someone didn't find her, we'd need a bigger search group—fast. The sun was already setting.

I pulled out my cell and turned back even though I hadn't gone the full five minutes I instructed everyone else to travel. The clearing where I'd parked the sleigh was my best chance for a cell signal. As soon as my cell picked up, I'd call the police. Better to bring them out on a false alarm than regret not calling them sooner.

A sharp wind bit into my cheeks, and I couldn't hold back the shiver. On second thought, I wasn't going to wait to find a cell signal. I'd use my walkie-talkie to call Russ back at the office. That meant any Sugarwood employee near a receiver would hear me, and the rumor that we'd lost a child would be all over Fair Haven before supper, but in this case, that might work in our favor if we did need more bodies to hunt for Riley.

I pressed the button on my walkie-talkie, then let it go. We didn't need more negative press for Sugarwood right now. People were still talking over the events of last month, and it'd shown in our decreased tour bookings. If Riley turned up, I'd have hurt out reputation again for nothing.

Instead of asking Russ to call the police, I could ask him to call Erik or Elise. Since they were my friends as well as members of Fair Haven's police force, Russ might get the message without everyone listening understanding what I was really asking for.

"Russ? I need you to contact Erik or Elise for me. Over."

His chuckle came through the walkie-talkie before his words. "You haven't found another body have you? Over."

Russ' current way of dealing with the loss of two of his friends within six months of each other was to completely deny he needed to deal with it. He didn't like to talk about it at all except to joke about how I seemed to constantly stumble upon corpses.

That wasn't the case this time, but he had taken away any chance of me being subtle. "No one's been hurt. We have a missing girl."

I stepped back into the clearing and checked my cell. Still no signal. I held it up in the air the way

Drew's girlfriend had been doing, but it didn't help. It'd been the right move to call Russ on the walkie-talkie rather than wait.

A black box at the base of one of the nearby trees caught my attention. It hadn't been there before we left. I turned for a better look.

Drew's camera.

I could hear Russ saying something to me from the walkie-talkie, but all I could think about was that Drew had the camera with him when he left the clearing. And that he'd never leave his camera lying in the snow. While I wasn't sure how much it was worth, professional cameras had to cost at least a few thousand. No one left expensive electronics sitting alone in the snow.

My throat felt tight and stiff, like cement hardening. This couldn't be happening again. No one ran into this many dead bodies. So there had to be another reason Drew's camera was on the ground. Maybe he'd slipped. The ground was icy in patches, and I'd face-planted more than I cared to admit. He might have fractured his ankle or knocked himself unconscious.

If something had happened, better I find him than the teenage girl or the father carrying his child. Either of them could return any minute now. Any of the tour guests could.

I tugged on the cuffs of my gloves, tried—and failed—to draw in a deep breath, and moved around the wagon.

Drew lay in the snow next to his camera, a stainless steel sap spout in his temple.

Chapter 2

Drew's empty eyes stared unblinkingly at me. Checking his pulse wouldn't make any difference. He was gone.

I couldn't possibly be this unlucky.

Guilt bloomed in my chest. He was the unlucky one. At least I was still alive.

And I had to pull myself together. Any minute now, the other tour guests would return to the clearing. They kids shouldn't see this.

I reached for one of the blankets we kept in the sleigh for the guests, but stopped before my fingers hit the fabric. As much as I might want to spare them, I couldn't cover Drew's body. It'd contaminate any evidence. I shouldn't even go near him since nothing I did could bring him back. Not with that much blood.

My head spun slightly. All that blood. I leaned against the sleigh. I needed to pull myself together and make sure Russ had called the police. Now we really did need them.

I grabbed my walkie-talkie. "Russ? Over." The two words shook more than I would have liked.

This time it was a curse rather than a laugh that preceded Russ' response out of the handset. "What's going on out there? I'm headed to you, and I got Elise. She's on her way with a couple of officers."

My breathing came a little easier. I hadn't realized it'd been such a struggle until my lungs loosened up and I could breathe normally again.

"Did you find the girl?" Russ asked.

A scream ripped through the air behind me. I swung around. Kristen stood at the far edge of the clearing, covering Riley's eyes with one hand, the other hand pressed over her own mouth.

At least they'd found Riley. That was clearly the only thing that was going right today.

By the time Russ led Elise and the other Fair Haven police officers into the clearing, everyone had returned except for Drew's girlfriend. I'd gathered everyone else in the sleigh so as to contaminate as little of the scene as possible.

I slid down and strode toward Elise and Russ, keeping my gaze away from where Drew lay. Seeing a body never got easier, no matter how many I was exposed to.

Russ' face was paler than usual, and his barrel-shaped body plowed through the snow directly for me. "What happened to *no body* this time?" The words barely seemed to make it out past his gritted teeth.

All I could do was shrug in reply. He passed by me and climbed up into the driver's seat of the sleigh.

Elise had her notepad out, and instead of giving me a hug, she gave me a look I couldn't interpret—her eyes a little too wide and darting in the direction of the other officers. Elise always tended to look like someone had put her freshly washed clothes into the freezer rather than the dryer, but today, each of her movements had an extra level of stiffness to them.

The first time we'd met, less than two months ago, had been in a similar situation. She'd been the responding officer, and she'd immediately suspected me because I'd been the one to discover Noah, our former groom-mechanic, unconscious and covered in blood. She'd even wrongly accused me of having a relationship with him. We'd sorted out a lot of misunderstandings since then, and I now counted her among my closest friends in Fair Haven, so I knew we couldn't be back to I-think-you're-the-murderer.

I also knew from when I'd shown her some of the photos Drew had already taken that she didn't know him. That meant it wasn't personal.

Out of the corner of my eye, I caught a glimpse of the other officers who'd come with her. The one closest to us was Quincey Dornbush. He looked past me without so much as a smile or any sign of recognition. Something was definitely up, more than just another body discovered by me.

I didn't recognize the third officer. Fair Haven had a larger police force than most small towns thanks to the way the population swelled in tourist season, but I still knew every officer on the force by sight. Turns out that tended to happen when you were dating the county medical examiner.

The third officer had to be the new police chief. His bearing definitely said *I'm in command here.* He had the same clean-shaven cheeks and short haircut of any other male officer, but his long face and narrow nose reminded me a bit of a fox. His gaze took in Drew's body, everyone gathered in the sleigh, and finally me.

The muscles at the edges of his eyes tightened. "The call we received said there was a missing child. This looks more like a murder."

Talk about getting off on the wrong foot. I was so far off I wasn't even sure the foot was mine by this point, and the way Elise and Quincey were acting suddenly seemed like a secret code flashing *Warning.*

Problem was, I didn't know what to watch out for. He'd been brought in to see if the corruption on the police force extended beyond the former chief and to clean up the problems that had shown up once the old chief was gone. So were Elise and Quincey worried I'd seem too friendly and bring them under suspicion from a man doing his job, or was the new chief a danger because he was looking for a scapegoat and didn't care who that might be?

I'd rather be safe and protect them. I kept my gaze steady on the new chief. "We went out looking for the missing girl. When we came back, I found Drew's body."

Nothing about his expression changed. "Was the girl found?"

I nodded.

"Has everyone returned from the search?"

All but one. Everyone else had been speculating about what had happened to Drew's girlfriend, but I'd been actively trying not to think about it. Trying not to think that she might also be dead somewhere out in the woods. Or that she might have been the one to hurt Drew. Even with my overly active imagination, I couldn't come up with any other reasons she wouldn't be here. It was a stretch even for me to think she'd fallen and sprained an ankle at the same time as someone else murdered her boyfriend.

I'd been calling her Drew's girlfriend in my mind because it reminded me why I hadn't ordered her to stay away, but we had been introduced. I knew her name. "Holly Northgate, Drew's girlfriend, hasn't come back yet."

I didn't believe she was coming back, but adding the *yet* gave her the benefit of the doubt at least. I didn't want to unfairly cast suspicion. For all I knew, she *could* be another victim.

"Dornbush." The new chief looked back over his shoulder. "Go back to the car, and call in Cavanaugh and the crime scene techs and a bigger team to look for Miss. Northgate. Scott, I want you to stay here with the body until they arrive."

Quincey got back on one of the snowmobiles. Elise's spine straightened further than I thought was possible for a human being, and for a second, I thought she might salute.

"Yes, sir," she said.

She moved a few feet toward Drew's body, but stayed far enough away to protect any footprints or other evidence.

The chief's expression still gave nothing away. It was like trying to read words covered over with permanent marker, but it told me more about him than he probably realized. He hadn't treated me like the murderer because I'd found the body. He hadn't hinted that Holly might have killed Drew. That suggested he didn't like to jump to conclusions, and he didn't want to give away what he was thinking because he suspected everyone until he had reason not to.

He poked his chin toward the sleigh. "Gather everyone here, please."

I waved for them to join us, and they piled out of the sleigh. The bitter wind had already turned Kristen's face splotchy, and the older man who'd stayed with his wife during the search rubbed his bare hands together and stamped his feet. Even the teenage girl huddled beside her dad for extra warmth—though it might also have been for comfort, considering she'd seen a dead body. Red rimmed her eyes like she'd been trying not to cry.

Kristen's husband—his name was Shawn—had zipped their little boy inside his jacket for extra warmth as soon as they'd gotten back to the sleigh, making him look like an overgrown kangaroo with a joey in its pouch, and Kristen had wrapped her scarf around his little face. I'd donated mine to help keep Riley warmer as well. She shivered in the circle of Kristen's arms.

We'd all been out here twice as long as expected. On a normal tour, we'd have been drinking hot chocolate and enjoying maple syrup treats at the sugar shack. Hopefully calling us together meant the chief would also let us go.

As soon as the group got within speaking distance, Shawn started chastising the chief about keeping his children out in the cold, and Kristen held his arm, clearly trying to calm him down. The teenage girl added something as well, but I couldn't catch the words, only the snark in her tone.

"I'm Chief Owen McTavish." The chief called over top of it all. "I need all of you to come with me."

I tapped the screen on my phone for the fifth time. Five thirty-six in the evening. I'd been alone in one of the interview rooms for nearly a half hour now, waiting for someone to take my statement. In a larger city, I would have thought the wait was some sort of delay tactic to shake me. Here, it was more likely that they simply didn't have enough officers to search for Holly, secure the scene, and talk to all the potential witnesses. At least I was finally warm.

But the delay could cause me a major problem. I'd taken Velma to the vet for her spay yesterday, and I needed to get her today before they closed at six or she'd be stuck there over the weekend. Mark had planned to pick me up right around now with his truck so she didn't have to squeeze into the back seat of my car.

I tapped his name from my contact list.

Are you still at the scene? I'm stuck at the station. What do we do about Velma?

I hit the send button.

The bar had barely zipped along the top of the screen, signaling that it was gone, before the door opened. Chief McTavish came in, carrying a small pile of files.

My mouth dried out and my tongue plastered itself to the bottom. The files couldn't be a good sign. He'd never bring statements from the tour guests into the room to take my statement. He hadn't seemed to suspect me earlier, and I couldn't imagine what anyone might have said to change that. So what was this about?

He seated himself across from me and gently laid the files down on the table in front of him.

For a full thirty seconds, he looked at me, like he was trying to invade my brain and pull the truth from me by telekinesis. "Miss. Fitzhenry-Dawes."

I opened my mouth to ask him to call me Nicole, but stopped before it came out. My instincts said that what other people would interpret as a gesture of goodwill, he'd see as me trying to create a sense of trust so that he wouldn't question me as carefully. I had nothing to hide, so I settled on, "Chief McTavish."

The twitch at the corners of his lips told me that he saw right through that as well. Not surprising, since he'd been sent here ostensibly due to his powers of observation and high moral character.

"I apologize for how long we've kept you here, but I ran into a problem when trying to assign an officer to take your statement. All of them had a conflict of interest." He folded his hands on top of the files. "Not only are you dating my county medical examiner, but it seems you also once dated Erik Higgins, and you and Dr. Cavanaugh now frequently socialize with Higgins and Elise Scott, who I recently discovered is also Dr. Cavanaugh's cousin."

A mixture of amusement, frustration, and befuddlement rolled across his face. As a newer resident myself, I knew how overwhelming it could be to step into the interconnections that tended to form in Fair Haven.

Since there hadn't yet been a question directed at me, though, I held my peace. For once, I think my parents would have approved. They were always telling me not to give the opposing side anything they didn't already have. And this was starting to feel a lot more like an interrogation about the condition of Fair Haven PD and a lot less like a statement-taking for Drew's murder.

The emotions cleared from his face. The look he gave me wasn't exactly unfriendly. Shrewd might have been the best descriptor. "My only other on-duty officer is Quincey Dornbush, and it seems he and his wife have also been to your home for dinner. I understand that small towns tend to create a situation where everyone knows everyone else, but you're not even originally from Fair Haven. You've managed to insert yourself deeply into my department in a very short period of time, Miss. Fitzhenry-Dawes."

And there it was. He'd been sent here to clean up any corruption on the Fair Haven police department, and he thought I might be a contributing factor.

Part of the tension building between my shoulder blades gave way. Now that I knew why I was being treated differently, I could at least manage the situation. Neither I nor anyone I'd befriended on the force were part of the corruption and cover-up that had happened under Chief Wilson's leadership. The sooner we cleared that up, the sooner he could focus on solving Drew's murder and finding out if anyone in the department was corrupt.

But what could I say that wouldn't increase his suspicion of me? Trading on Uncle Stan's name wouldn't work the way it had in the past. Chief McTavish was an outsider.

Perhaps that was the answer. He was questioning my relationships because I'd only moved to Fair Haven a few months ago. "My uncle lived in Fair Haven for ten years before his death, so when I took over his maple syrup farm, I also inherited his friendships in a sense."

Chief McTavish opened the top file. "His murder was the first investigation you took part in here in Fair Haven?"

I laid my gloves on the table and smoothed them flat. I hadn't done anything wrong, but I suddenly felt guilty. "Yes."

"If it wasn't for the fact that you weren't in town when he died, I might have suspected you of orchestrating these murders because you wanted the glory of solving them. But then in two of the three cases, the murderer confessed." His voice had hardened. "So it seems you only inserted yourself into the investigations after the fact."

When I'd first returned to Fair Haven and helped investigate the murder of the local animal shelter manager, I'd technically been a consultant, not a nosy civilian, but mentioning that to Chief McTavish didn't seem prudent. Plus, it might get Erik in trouble.

At the same time, I wasn't about to let Chief McTavish chastise me for helping solve murders that might otherwise have gone unsolved—like my uncle's. I wasn't my parents' daughter for nothing. We might fight on different sides anymore, but their genetics still built my backbone. "I passed along information that the police found useful in all those cases, yes."

He spread the file folders out. There were four. He tapped the first three with his pointer finger. "The department appreciates your help on these three cases, but I want to be clear that we'll be handling this new case"—he hit the fourth file with his finger and kept it there—"without civilian involvement."

Civilian. Technically, that's what I was. I wasn't a police officer. I didn't have any special skills that necessitated the department hiring me as a permanent consultant. I shouldn't be involved in any more police cases. A normal person shouldn't even want to be involved. Isn't that why I'd come here? To escape from a life full of criminals?

But my chest felt a little hollow at the thought, like I couldn't remember where I'd put something important and urgent.

"Are we clear?" Chief McTavish asked, his gaze firm and unyielding.

"We're clear," I said softly.

My phone beeped with a text message notification. My fingers itched to check it because the vet's office was going to close any minute, but I could guess what Chief McTavish's reaction would be if I did.

He opened the fourth file folder and pulled out a picture. He slid it across the table to me. "Now that we're on the same page, I have a few questions for you about what happened today. Do you recognize these gloves?"

The picture showed a close-up of blue-and-white striped gloves. They were stained with red. "Where did you find these?"

I realized my mistake as soon as the words were out of my mouth.

Chief McTavish gave me the slow you're-not-listening head shake. "I thought we understood one another."

Right. I wasn't allowed to ask questions because I was a witness like any other. They answered questions. They didn't ask them.

I glanced at the picture again. They were too small for men's gloves. I closed my eyes and saw Holly with her cell phone in the air, waving it around trying to catch a signal. I opened my eyes. "They're Holly Northgate's."

Chapter 3

If unfulfilled curiosity killed the cat, then my nine lives were about to run out. It took another half hour before Chief McTavish finished listening to my statement about the afternoon and discovering Drew's body. He didn't show me any other pictures, and his other questions didn't even hint at what they suspected had happened. Through the whole interview, I wanted to ask about whether they'd found Holly yet, but I knew what my answer would be. None of my business.

I headed to the lobby. It was empty except for the receptionist at the front desk, and I didn't have a ride home. Like everyone else, I'd come in a cruiser, and it seemed Fair Haven's officers were out returning the others to Sugarwood and their cars.

I'd have to call someone for a ride. Technically, Chief McTavish should have assigned someone to take me home, but I certainly wasn't going groveling to him for anything. I'd rather walk.

Pride goes before destruction, a tiny voice in the back of my head whispered. If the reprimand had come from a real person, at least I could have made a face at them. Since it was my own conscience, all I could do was reluctantly admit I was being petty. It shouldn't have even bothered me as much as it did to be excluded from the investigation.

I pulled out my phone, and it blinked at me, reminding me I still had a waiting text message from Mark.

Velma's with me. We'll be out front when you're done.

I smiled at my phone. I should have known not to worry about how I'd get home.

Mark's new black truck waited by the curb. I climbed in and leaned over for a kiss. A whine came from the backseat.

Mark's lips quirked up, showing off the dimple that always sent a warm flare through my stomach. "I think she's jealous," he said.

I settled back in my seat and stuck my fingers through the protective grate that turned Mark's backseat into a giant doggy crate. Velma pressed her nose to my hand. "She's always jealous when she's not the center of attention."

Having two dogs helped me better understand what having two children would be like. They played together, napped together, and sometimes even happily shared their toys, but when it came to having my attention, they both wanted it all for themselves.

I leaned my head back onto the headrest. Suddenly, all I wanted was to get home and be with my dogs. Now that I wasn't out in the woods, managing missing children or dead bodies, and I wasn't being questioned by a police chief who disliked how connected I was to his department, all my energy seemed to leak out of my pores and evaporate in the warmth from the truck heater.

Mark pulled out onto the road and headed for Sugarwood. He looked at me sidelong. "Bad day. Should I stop for food?"

I nodded. As much as I wanted to become a better cook, I didn't enjoy cooking, and on days like today, preparing dinner was akin to torture. Now baking, that was different. That was worth it because I ended up with something sweet at the end. "Do you know if they found Holly Northgate?"

"Not yet. The chief issued a BOLO—be on the lookout. She's either turned off her phone or destroyed it, because they're not able to locate it."

That confirmed what I'd suspected. They assumed Holly had killed Drew. Based on the gloves and how isolated we were in the bush, the case looked simple enough, especially since I couldn't think of a reason why an innocent person would also make sure they couldn't be tracked through their phone.

Except that I'd been around Drew and Holly for days. They'd been a bit immature—more Holly than Drew—but otherwise, they'd seemed happy together. Nothing I'd seen suggested she'd want to hurt Drew. If she'd done it, it must have been in a fit of passion. Perhaps she hadn't even meant to kill him.

Mark parallel parked in a spot in front of A Salt & Battery. I didn't even have to tell him what to order anymore. He knew they had my favorite fish and chips, better even than any I'd had in DC. After a rough day like today, my desire to eat healthy was always going to be trumped by the part of my brain that wanted comfort food.

I closed my eyes. The truck door opening again and two takeout containers landing in my lap told me Mark had returned.

The extra warmth helped chase off any vestiges of a chill. It didn't help chase away the malaise I felt inside. "I'm starting to feel a bit like an angel of death. Murders have gone up something like three hundred percent since I got here."

A hand squeezed mine. "It's not you. Chief McTavish has me looking over some old cases from before I moved back to Fair Haven. He suspects that former Chief Wilson failed to properly investigate more than one case, labeling it an accident or a suicide when it might not have been."

That probably shouldn't have made me feel better, but it did. At least I hadn't cursed the town.

I opened my eyes and planted a kiss on the back of Mark's hand. Uncle Stan's death had been one of the worst things that could have happened to me, and paradoxically also one of the best. It brought me here, where I'd been happier than I could remember.

He gave my hand another squeeze and then returned both hands to the wheel. "I'll be by to pick you up tomorrow at 11:30."

I barely stopped myself from bonking my head back against the headrest. With everything that had happened today, I'd forgotten all about the welcome-home lunch for Mark's parents. It'd be my first time meeting them.

My first time meeting any parents of a boyfriend. My previous boyfriend had been my only serious boyfriend, and he'd never introduced me to his parents. The omission made sense in hindsight since I found out, after his wife died, that he'd been married the whole time we were dating. You didn't exactly introduce your mistress to your parents.

I picked at the edge of the takeout container. Mark would believe me if I claimed I wasn't up to it because of what happened today. But I'd be lying to him, and I'd have to meet his parents sometime. At least, I'd have to meet them sometime assuming we were going

to have a future together. Even though we'd been dating for over a month, he hadn't said *I love you* yet.
Neither had I. Not because I didn't feel it, but because I
was such a big chicken it was surprising I didn't cluck
when I laughed.

I wanted a future with him, and not one built on
lies. "I'll be ready."

"Are you still able to bring a dessert? I know today
didn't go the way you planned."

Crap. Not only had I forgotten about the dinner, I'd
forgotten I was supposed to put something together for
dessert. Mark's sister-in-law Megan had asked me a
week ago.

Your case is half won or half lost on the first impression, my dad used to say.

I wasn't going to have Mark's parents' first impression of me be that I couldn't be counted on to follow
through on my promises. "Of course."

Now I just had to pray I could reach Nancy, the
woman in charge of all Sugarwood's additional maple
syrup products, and that she had a dazzling maple syrup recipe I could make with what I had in my sadly
neglected cupboards.

The face that looked back at me in the mirror the
next morning reminded me too much of Toby's sunk-
en-eyed, jowly Bullmastiff face for comfort. Served me
right for staying up until only vampire bats were

awake, trying to perfect the maple syrup butter tart recipe Nancy gave me. Maybe homemade baked goods weren't intended to look like store bought. My lopsided butter tarts tasted fantastic—maple-flavored and not overly sweet—but they gave new meaning to the phrase *hot mess*.

I let the dogs out of their crates. Velma bounced off the door and ran into a wall, her cone-covered head wagging from side to side. The look on her face clearly said *Am I being punished for eating your shoes?*

I scratched under the cone edge. "It's only until your incision heals. I promise."

If a dog could give me a skeptical eyebrow raise, I would have sworn Velma did.

After feeding them and taking them out for a bathroom break, I flipped open my laptop. The email at the top listed the sender as Stacey Rathmell, and the subject line said *Rejected Credit Card*.

Along with taking on the role of Sugarwood's live-in mechanic, Stacey had also taken on the role of bookkeeper shortly after I hired her. She said she'd enjoyed doing it for her dad's auto shop, and that she wanted to make sure she could still be a valuable employee once her pregnant belly got big enough to prevent her from climbing around under the machinery. I think in my excitement I may have tossed the responsibility at her so quickly that if they'd been actual ledgers I would have knocked her unconscious.

Thankfully, she'd proven more than capable. It'd been weeks since she'd even had a question for me.

I clicked open the email.

Dave left a note on my desk that one of the guests on yesterday's tour had a declined credit card. They were supposed to come back after the tour and remedy it. No show. It was for two tickets. Want me to pursue it?

She included the name of the guest with the declined card. If my memory didn't fail me, George Powers was the father with the teenage daughter.

Amazingly, Stacey must not have heard the news yet. Or, more likely, she was being discreet. Her dad was the same way.

Normally I would have told her to pursue payment since we were a business, not a charity. This time, they'd probably forgotten about fixing the payment glitch because they'd been hauled down to the police station to answer questions about a murder. Plus, they hadn't gotten the tour they'd tried to pay for. I should refund everyone or offer them a make-up tour. Perhaps both.

I sent Stacey a quick reply telling her to let it go and explaining what had happened. If she hadn't heard, better the truth come from me than having her fed the rumors and speculation that'd soon circulate around Fair Haven. She'd find out anyway when we had to rectify the shorted tour for the other guests.

I ended it with a soft chastisement about working on a weekend. During the peak season, we all worked long hours, but the leaves were coming out on the trees now, which meant no more sap collection. According to what I'd learned about maple syrup production, the sap turned bitter as soon as the trees budded.

Her almost immediate reply told me she was still at her computer.

Working is better than being alone with my thoughts.

I made a mental note to invite her over for dinner again soon. It was easy to forget how hard being an eighteen-year-old soon-to-be-single-mom must be on her. She needed me as a friend even more than she needed the job I'd given her.

My doorbell rang, setting off a cacophony of barking. The decibel level of two large-breed barking dogs was enough to burst an eardrum. The dog trainer who ran Velma's obedience classes said telling them to be quiet never worked because to a dog it sounded like you were barking along with them. Distract them, he said.

I'd like to see him try to distract a Great Dane and a Bullmastiff protecting their home. Short of throwing them each one of my butter tarts, there wasn't anything they wanted more than to bark at whoever came to my door.

I glanced at the clock. It was only nine o'clock, so it wasn't Mark. Besides, they'd finally adapted to the sound of his new truck. When he came to the door, they knew it was him, and the greeting was wagging tails and excited whines, not warning barks.

Since I hadn't yet showered, I was still in my fuzzy bathrobe and floppy slippers. Not exactly fit for company, but I wasn't going to leave someone standing out in the cold, either.

I peeked out the front window before answering the door—a throwback to my former life in the city and a consequence of how many people had tried to kill me in the last six months. A woman stood on the other side.

I opened the door. Toby and Velma surged forward. I stuck out my leg to block them. Toby stopped in time. Velma didn't. Her cone rammed straight into my thigh. That was going to leave a bruise.

The woman on my front step jerked backward. She looked to be around fifty and carried a few more pounds than I was sure she would have liked, exactly how I expected I'd look at her age after I'd had a couple of kids. Maybe sooner if I didn't lay off the sweets. She wore the type of medium-weight coat that Michiganders considered sufficient for March and I thought shouldn't even be brought out of the closet until May.

"Can I help you?" I shouted over the barking.

She held a hand up to her ear. No wonder. I could barely hear myself.

I tightened the belt of my bathrobe and stepped outside, closing the door behind me. It muffled the barking enough that we could at least hear each other.

"Are you Nicole Dawes?" she asked.

Even after months of living here, it still surprised me when someone shortened my last name and simply called me Nicole Dawes, the part of my name I'd shared with my Uncle Stan. Hopefully my mother would never hear about it.

I nodded.

She thrust a hand toward me. What looked to be a small blue square dangled in a clear plastic sandwich baggy. "Drew would have wanted you to have this."

And then, before I could so much as reach for the bag to figure out exactly what he would have wanted me to have, she burst into tears.

Chapter 4

One of the most uncomfortable feelings in the world was watching someone else cry without knowing how to help them.

I put an arm around her and ushered her into my house, where at least her tears wouldn't freeze on her cheeks. Whether I startled the dogs or they sensed something was wrong, I couldn't be sure, but they both backed off. Toby whined softly deep in his throat, and his ears slumped back against his head, making him look mournful.

I pointed at their beds behind the woman's back and mouthed the words *go* and *stay*. Toby went to his and laid down. Velma stood on hers, technically fulfilling my command, but kept on her feet, staring at us out of her satellite cone. If she were a human, I suspected she'd be a teenager, testing her boundaries.

The woman flopped down onto one of my kitchen counter stools, and the baggy landed on the counter next to her. She fished around in her pockets and came up with a handful of tissues. Based on their droopy state, I suspected none of them were clean.

I grabbed the kettle from my stove top. "Would you like a cup of coffee? Tea?"

That was the best I could come up with for something to say. *Counselor* could safely be crossed off my list of potential future careers if I ever stopped working at Sugarwood.

She nodded as her only answer and blew her nose. Which didn't actually help me since she hadn't told me what choice she'd prefer. I put the kettle on and started the coffee pot as well.

I moved around the counter and took the seat next to her. The sandwich bag contained what looked like an SD card with the letters SW written on it. For Sugarwood, presumably. She'd said Drew would have wanted me to have it, and the only thing I could imagine Drew wanting me to have were the pictures he'd taken of Sugarwood.

My throat felt like I'd taken a judo chop to my trachea. Good Lord, was this Drew's mother? Her age would be about right. She didn't look much like Drew, but I suspected based on its uniformity that her blonde hair was dyed, and Drew could have taken after his father. Now that we were sitting close together rather than standing out in the cold, I could see that her eyes had the puffy, bloodshot look of someone who'd been crying for hours.

She snuffled again, and I dragged a box of tissues closer and nudged them toward her. Nothing I could say would make her feel better if she was a woman who'd lost her son less than a day ago, so I stayed quiet. It was the only way I knew to show respect for her grief.

"The police took most of Drew's things, his phone, his computer." She dropped her used tissues into a pile on my counter and pulled out another handful from the box, but she held them clumped together in her fist rather than using them. "I found the memory card tucked into a file with your contract. He was so talented. I wanted his work to make it out into the world."

Her voice had the hollow note to it I'd heard before in people whose minds were struggling with denial of the truth and whose hearts felt like a piece had been gouged out of it.

The SD card she'd brought me must be the one Drew replaced in his camera the day before his death. Drew had already given me a disk containing all the images he'd taken prior to yesterday. She didn't need to know that, though. Right now, she simply needed to feel like a piece of her son would live on in his work. She needed to know he'd be remembered.

I pulled the sandwich bag toward me. "Thank you. His work...it was some of the best I've ever seen, and I grew up in Washington, DC, so that's saying something."

She gave a sharp bob of her head, like that was all she could manage in acknowledgment.

The kettle whistled. I hopped up and pulled it off the burner. The only tea I had in the house was chamomile. I hated tea, but Mark claimed it would help me relax and sleep better so I wouldn't have to keep using sleeping pills to deal with my bouts of insomnia. They'd gotten worse since my recent near-death experiences.

Something calming might be perfect for Drew's mom. I dropped a tea bag into the cup, poured hot water over it, and slid it toward her along with my little pot of honey.

She stirred the cup of tea without seeming to actually see it. "He wanted to be a photojournalist. Did you know that? He was trying to save up enough money for college, for him and Holly both. They had such big—"

Her voice clogged, garbling the rest of her sentence, but I could guess what she was going to say. They'd had such big dreams.

It didn't sound like Drew's mother knew Holly was the prime suspect in his murder. I certainly wasn't going to be the one to tell her and cause her more pain, especially since I wasn't even supposed to know about it. I also wouldn't be able to answer any of the questions she'd surely have. That news, when it came, should come from the police.

She raised her gaze to mine.

I had to say something, but everything that came to mind seemed much too shallow. Drew was such a nice guy. I'm sorry for your loss. He'll be missed.

She'd hear enough of those in the coming days. Perhaps what I could give her was someone who wasn't afraid to talk about him. That might soon be rare. "He did tell me. An employee of mine recommended him, but one of the reasons I hired him was I knew he wanted to pay for school. He would have made an excellent photojournalist. The angles in his photography were so fresh, and he noticed things that no one else seemed to."

She snuffled again and added to the Mt. Everest-sized pile of tissues in front of her. "He always did." She pointed at the butter tarts on my cooling rack. "May I?"

I brought some over on a plate, and the next thing I knew she was telling me stories about Drew as a little boy, Drew with his first camera, Drew always wondering about the private lives of the people they'd see in the mall or at a restaurant. As if maybe the real reason she'd come was because she needed a place to share her memories of Drew without having to bear the burden of someone else's sadness. So she could let her own grief out without having to be strong for anyone else.

Maybe that was the real reason my dad refused to come to my Uncle Stan's funeral. Maybe he was afraid that he wouldn't have been able to stay strong in front of me, strong for me.

Or maybe I was still trying to turn my father into the kind of man he could never be because every little girl needed her dad to be her hero rather than the man who was so disappointed in her life choices that he hadn't spoken to her in months.

A knock sounded at my door. You'd think I'd put out a sign advertising free coffee from the traffic my house was getting today.

I braced myself for the barking, but instead Toby's tail whapped on his bed and Velma pranced in place. Only one person other than me got a happy dance when she'd been ordered to stay.

My gaze shot to the clock on my oven. 11:30 on the dot.

My door swung open, and Mark's voice entered ahead of him. "I thought I was going to be late because I had to go in to work this morning, but—"

Velma's self-control snapped, and she bounded toward him. Her cone clipped the end table by my couch, and the lamp and table both went over with a crash. Velma leaped backward, trampling on Toby. He lunged out of her way and took out the end table at the other end of the couch—the one where my still-full mug from this morning sat. It shattered on the floor in an explosion of ceramic and cold coffee.

If this morning signaled how the rest of the day was going to go, I had a better chance of feeling warm during a Michigan winter than I did of winning the approval of Mark's parents.

Chapter 5

"We're only an hour late," Mark said as we pulled into Grant and Megan's driveway.

They were supposed to pick Mark and Grant's parents from the Grand Rapids airport that morning and bring them back here for a welcome-home luncheon with the family.

In my parents' world, a minute late was an equal infraction to standing them up. If I'd ever arrived to anything an hour late...the consequences didn't bear thinking about. I crossed my fingers that time ran slower up north. The pace of everything else certainly seemed to.

Mark took the container of butter tarts off my lap. At least my extra batches had come in handy. Even with what Drew's mom—whose first name I never did get—ate, I had plenty left to bring with us.

I scrubbed at the dog slobber smear on my dark jeans with the corner of my coat sleeve. I'd chosen these pants specifically to go along with my flowy eggplant-colored blouse because they said *I took care with my appearance* without saying *I'm overdressed and trying too hard*. Or, at least, that's what they said without doggie drool down the front. Now all they said was *you should buy your son an eHarmony subscription*.

The dried drool refused to budge. I sighed and slid out of the truck. Maybe they wouldn't notice it right away. If Grant and Megan had a big dog too, Mark's parents might even think it'd drooled on me. Please God, let them have a dog.

Mark met up with me on the front walk and took my hand. "I texted Grant to let him know we'd be late. I didn't get a reply, but they'll understand once I explain about your unexpected visitor and the dog hurricane that hit your house."

I wasn't sure how he expected to make this morning sound anything other than made up, but they were his parents, so I'd have to trust him.

Mark didn't bother knocking. He just walked right in. Which made sense on one level, considering it was his brother's house and the rest of the family should already be there, and on another level made me feel like I was barging in where I didn't belong.

We dropped our shoes and coats by the front door, and before I could move farther into the house, a fluffy golden Chihuahua streaked across the floor, its barks more like yaps compared to Velma and Toby. It skidded to a stop two feet from me, its whole front end lifting from the floor with each bark.

When I'd prayed they had a dog, this wasn't what I had in mind. The most the little guy was going to drool on was my sock.

Mark handed the butter tarts back to me, scooped the dog up with one hand, and tucked him under his arm. The dog stopped barking and started trying to lick Mark's face instead. "Nikki, meet Chewbacca. Chewie, meet Nikki."

I would have loved to have Mark's ability to arc an eyebrow right about now. The dog couldn't have weighed more than three or four pounds. He was smaller than Toby's head. "Chewbacca?"

"Grant thought it was ironic."

"You could say that."

"They're here," Elise's voice called from somewhere deeper in the house. She came through an open archway down the hall, pulling her dark hair into a bun as she walked. "We thought you might have decided not to come after Grant's text."

Mark still had Chewie tucked under one arm, and the dog seemed perfectly happy to stay there. "I didn't get a text from Grant."

"He tried to group text, so I'm not surprised. Your parents' flight ended up cancelled last minute due to mechanical problems with the plane. They're hoping to be able to get another one tomorrow, but no set plans yet. Grant wanted everyone to come anyway since they had all the food ready."

The relief that flooded through me felt a lot like a sugar rush, a little too giddy to be healthy. I'd get a second chance after all to make a first impression—hopefully one that didn't involve dog drool and acting like the batteries died in our watches.

Erik came through the same arched doorway behind Elise, and I nearly dropped my butter tarts. We'd all gone out together as friends regularly since Mark and I started dating, but as far as I knew, Elise and Erik weren't a couple yet. And attendance at a family function definitely said *we're dating*, though perhaps not in Cavanaugh language. This family ran on a very different system, sort of like trying to move to a Mac when you'd been running a PC your whole life.

Still, I squished up my lips and gave Elise an is-there-something-I-should-know look.

She leaned in like she wanted to see what was in my butter tart container. "It's not what you think," she said in a hissed whisper. "I thought he might like a nice meal on his day off."

"Uh huh, and next you'll be telling me that people mistake Chewbacca and Toby for twins."

Erik stopped a respectful distance outside of Elise's intimate relationship personal space bubble. I'd have to try not to tease Elise—much—but I finally understood why every woman in a happy relationship seemed to turn into a matchmaker. The desire to have your friends share that same kind of happiness was harder to resist than double-chocolate chunk cookies. Based on what she'd told me about her first husband, who'd abandoned her and the kids, Elise deserved some happiness, and Erik was as dependable as they came.

But I could also see why she'd be a bit gun shy, especially since they also worked together.

Erik pointed with a thumb back over his shoulder. "Megan's putting together some sandwiches for us to take with us."

Chewie finally started to wiggle in Mark's grip, and Mark let him down. "You're leaving already? We're not that late. You've been later to church."

"It's not that." Elise made a face at Mark like they were still children. "The Harris and Northgate homes were burglarized while they were gone this morning. The chief's calling in all off-duty officers to help with the investigation given the connection between the murder yesterday and the two families."

The butter tart container sagged in my grip, and I righted it just before all the contents crashed together at one end, turning them into butter crumble.

"Drew Harris' mom was with me this morning," I blurted. "Holly Northgate wouldn't have broken in to her own house or Drew's."

I wasn't supposed to be even flirting with the edges of this case, but unless Chief McTavish had developed ESP, he never needed to know about this conversation. And I wasn't really inserting myself into the investigation. This was a simple conversation with friends.

Friends who shouldn't be talking to you about it, my conscience said.

"Does this mean the chief will be considering other suspects?" I asked to drown it out.

Erik slid on his coat. "It doesn't sound like it. The chief put me in charge of the situation because he's interviewing a witness who claims to have seen Holly and Drew arguing a couple days before his murder. I suspect he'll be issuing a warrant for Holly's arrest soon."

It'd bothered me that there wasn't a motive or some sign that Holly and Drew hadn't been getting along as well as it seemed. Now I had it. "Still, Chief McTavish must find the timeline of the two events suspicious."

"Not necessarily."

There was something in the way Erik said it, like a warning he didn't want to have to directly speak. He knew. He knew I wasn't supposed to be involving myself in this case.

He handed Elise her coat, edged around us, and opened the front door in a clear *conversation's over* gesture.

"The new chief's a bit...crusty," Elise said, picking up where Erik stopped and speaking over her shoulder as he ushered her for the door. It seemed like she didn't recognize the look Erik gave me and didn't know about the warning I'd received. "But he understands how bad press around a tourist town could destroy it. We've kept it out of the news, but there've been more break-ins than usual the past couple of months. The working theory is it's high school kids looking for thrills or extra cash. Drew and Holly lived in the same neighborhood. The murder and the break-ins might not be related at all."

She started to say something else, but Erik reached around her and closed the door.

I had the desire to pout even though I knew it was petty. It shouldn't bother me to not be a part of another murder case.

But it did.

Chapter 6

Over the next twenty-four hours, I must have thought about texting Elise to ask about the case at least twenty times. Managing to resist felt a little like I'd been able to stick my tongue out at Chief McTavish. I wasn't inserting myself in where I didn't belong. Though the knowledge that I was proud of myself for accomplishing something that shouldn't have even been a struggle took a little bit of the poof out of my fluffed-up ego.

After church, before Mark and I took the dogs for a walk, I tried to call Nancy to thank her for the butter tart recipe and tell her that they were a success. She didn't answer. Instead of leaving a message, I decided to wait for Monday and swing by our "bakery," what we called the room in the sugar shack where Nancy turned our maple syrup into maple butter and maple sugar.

On Monday morning, I had an email from Stacey waiting for me, asking what I'd like to do about refunding the tour that got cut short, and a text from Russ, saying that Nancy had called in sick with a cold.

Do you know if she lives alone? I texted back.

Think so. Husband passed away about 5 years ago.

The few tasks I had to take care of around Sugarwood today, including meeting with Stacey, could wait. The best way I could think of to say *thank you* to Nancy was to pay it forward by making her sick day a little easier. Everyone deserved to have someone take care of them when they were sick.

I picked up a box of tissues and a package of throat lozenges from the pharmacy and a take-out container of chicken-and-rice soup from The Burnt Toast Café and drove to the address Russ had given me.

I rang the bell, but no one answered. Nancy didn't strike me as the type to fake an illness to get a day off work, but she might have gone to the doctor's office. If she didn't answer, I'd be having soup for lunch.

I pushed the doorbell again.

This time, the lace curtain on the door shifted slightly.

I cringed. I hadn't thought this through. I'd probably gotten her out of bed.

The door edged open halfway. Nancy had the red nose that I expected from someone fighting a cold, but instead of pajamas or a bathrobe, she had on a flour-covered apron. She'd pulled her silver hair back in a French braid like she wore when working in the bakery at Sugarwood, and an oven mitt dangled from her free hand.

Her mouth hung open a touch. "Nicole? Didn't Russ tell you I wasn't able to make it in today?"

I held up the drugstore package, then realized she couldn't see through the white paper bag to know what was inside. The takeout soup container was equally unlabeled. "I brought you a few things to help you feel better."

"To help me feel better?" she echoed in an *are we talking about the same thing?* tone.

Unless my sense of people had gone haywire, she wasn't sick. "Russ said you had a cold."

"No." Nancy rubbed the space above her eyebrow. "I just wasn't ready to come in today. Holly Northgate is my great niece."

Whether she'd told Russ she had a cold to hide the real reason or he'd merely assumed didn't much matter. I'd been in her place once. It was hard to face people when someone you cared about was accused of murder. The looks and the whispers made you wonder how you could have missed it. Did you miss it? Was there something you could have done to stop it?

"When I was back in Virginia, my boyfriend was accused of murder." I decided to leave out the part that the murder he was accused of was his wife's. Even though I didn't know he was married, I'd rather the rumor didn't get around Fair Haven that I was an adulteress. "Take whatever time you need."

Something almost like hope flickered across Nancy's face. "Would you come in for a few minutes?"

I'd come here to help her. Even though that help looked different from how I'd imagined, I still wanted to do whatever I could to make her feel better. If that meant sitting with her all day, I'd do it. I nodded and followed her inside.

Nancy's house smelled like burnt cookie dough. A fluffy orange-and-white cat wound around my legs, and a tabby cat blinked at me from the back of the sofa as Nancy led me through her living room and into the kitchen.

Her kitchen looked like a classroom of kids had a food fight and refused to clean up afterward. A bag of flour lay knocked over on the counter, eggshells filled the drainage rack in the sink, and a baking pan of blackened muffins rested on top of the stove. The adorable round table in the breakfast nook practically groaned underneath the breads, cookies, and cupcakes.

To bake all of this, she couldn't possibly have slept. Or maybe she hadn't been able to sleep and this was how she coped with all the thoughts running through her head. I knew how that felt, too.

Nancy pulled out a chair and motioned me toward it. I obeyed. There wasn't even room on the table for me to put the soup, so I balanced it on my lap and dropped the pharmacy bag on the floor.

"She couldn't have done it," Nancy said softly. "I know everyone must say that, but I know my Holly. She's a little flighty, but she has a soft heart. She's a vegetarian. There's no way she could kill a person."

Nancy must not watch the news very often. Plenty of people who wouldn't hurt an animal had no qualms about taking a human life.

But she seemed to need someone to listen without judging, kind of like Drew's mom.

Her oven timer dinged, and she pulled out two round cake pans. Chocolate cake, by the smell of it.

She must have realized that every surface in the kitchen was already full because she shoved them back in the oven, closed the door, and turned the oven off.

She peeled off the red-and-yellow checkered oven mitts that matched her apron. "Could you talk to someone? About Holly. Tell them that she couldn't have done this."

An image flashed across my mind of me barging into Chief McTavish's office and demanding he investigate a different suspect. It wasn't actually that hard to imagine given my track record, but Chief McTavish wasn't former Chief Wilson, and he wasn't Erik as interim chief. He'd specifically warned me to stay away from this case.

I rose to my feet and left the soup container where I'd been sitting. I took Nancy's hand. "I don't know if that would make a difference."

"You're practically a Cavanaugh. They'll listen to you."

Apparently, I was the only woman Mark had dated since the death of his wife. In a town like this, that meant we might as well have skipped the dating and eloped. I didn't personally think dating Mark gave me any more clout than Nancy would have after living here her whole life, but Nancy was looking at me with an almost child-like faith.

I'd seen people look at my Uncle Stan that way for years, and somehow he managed to rarely let them down. I couldn't promise her results, at least not Uncle Stan-level results, but I could at least try. "I can mention what you told me to Mark and Elise."

The smile Nancy gave me made me think about the kind runners wore at the end of a marathon, hands braced on their knees, exhausted and relieved, and I had a suspicion she'd finally stop baking after I left and take a nap.

"Could you call them now?" she asked. "Then I'll at least have some hope to give to my niece when I talk to her again later."

I took my phone out into her living room. I'd start with Mark.

"You have that I'm-going-to-make-a-request-you're-not-going-to-like tone to your voice," he said after I asked how his day was going. "Should I be worried?"

"I don't think so." I bit down on my bottom lip. "Maybe a little." I told him about Nancy's description of Holly and her character. "I know the chief seems to think all the evidence points to Holly, but could you ask Elise to double check that no one else had a motive? It'd mean a lot to Nancy and her niece."

"Chief McTavish took Elise off the case."

Only the knowledge that Nancy was one room away and I might give her a heart attack if I screeched *what!* helped me keep the exclamation in check. "But she was the responding officer, and this is the perfect case for an officer who needs more experience."

Mark's pause was much too long. "He would have taken Erik off the case, too, if Quincey wasn't already investigating the hit-and-run of that biker last week. The chief overheard Elise and Erik talking on Saturday about how they'd come from Grant's place, and he asked them outright if they'd discussed anything about the case with you."

Oh. Crap. By-the-book Erik wouldn't lie even if it cost him his career. My heart beat so hard in my chest it felt like it would bruise. "How much trouble are they in?"

"So far he just took Elise off the case and threatened to suspend them without pay if they shared case details with unauthorized persons again."

Geez. If I'd had any doubts about Chief McTavish's seriousness before, he'd just drawn and quartered them. And it was at least partly my fault that Elise and Erik were already blacklisted by their new boss. They'd catered to my curiosity about the case. "Should I call Elise and apologize?"

I could almost feel Mark shake his head even though I couldn't see it. "She didn't even want you to know. She knew you'd feel guilty."

Guilt is what I would have felt if I'd spilled grape juice on her white dress. This was more like shame. "I'll still give her a call later, and I'll tell Nancy that there's not anything we can do except let the police investigate and hope for the best."

Another long pause. Long enough this time that if I'd been talking to anyone else, I would have thought they forgot to stay goodbye before hanging up.

"I don't know how much help this will be, since you can't tell Nancy or her niece any of this," Mark finally said, "but the chief knows there are holes in the case against Holly. Based on the results of the autopsy, the spike came from a downward angle, suggesting the killer was taller than Drew. Unless Holly Northgate snacked on an Alice in Wonderland 'Eat Me' cake, I don't think she could have grown by five or more inches in the few minutes she would have had to kill Drew. Holly either had an accomplice or she isn't the killer."

Chapter 7

I sat in silence for almost a minute after ending the call with Mark. He was right. I couldn't even give Nancy hope by hinting at the holes in the case against Holly. Fair Haven was too small a town. Even if all I said was something vague like *They say it's not an open-and-shut case*, Nancy might tell that to her niece, and her niece might tell someone else, and by the end of the week, half the people I loved in this town would be out of a job.

The sound of the electric mixer in the kitchen stopped, and the creak of the oven door opening again followed it. Nancy came from the kitchen with a fresh glop of something on her apron and the smell of bananas hanging around her. Baking must be how she dealt with stress.

She sat on the couch next to me. "What did they say?"

I reached for her hand again and she let me take it. It was the only thing I could do to let her know she wasn't alone and hopeless, even though it might seem like it. "The police are going to investigate fairly."

Nancy twisted her oven mitt. "I don't think that's enough. Police make mistakes. Judges make mistakes. And innocent people like Holly pay for them. Look at Russ and how he almost went to prison for murdering your Uncle Stan."

If my dad was right, innocent people went to prison a lot less than the news media would have us believe. Nancy wasn't entirely wrong, either, though. It did occasionally happen. "Once they find Holly, if they still charge her with Drew's murder, you'll be able to hire her a good lawyer to argue her case."

"Will you do it?" Nancy squeezed my hand so hard I felt the bones move. "I'd be willing to hire you right now so you can start building a defense for her."

I'd walked into that one. She might have even thought I was implying I wanted the case. "I'm not really a lawyer anymore."

"You defended Bonnie."

How could I explain to Nancy without going into all the things in my past that I wanted to leave behind? Defending people I knew were guilty used to eat away a part of my soul. I couldn't risk that Holly actually had killed Drew with an accomplice. I didn't want to ever defend someone I knew was guilty again. It was like spitting in the face of the victim's family. "Bonnie was a special case. I wasn't defending her. I helped negotiate her plea deal."

"Then do that for Holly. If she's innocent, you can defend her. If she's guilty, we'll convince her to take a plea deal like Bonnie did. She'll tell me the truth once we find her."

The part of me that wanted everyone to like me, urged me to just say yes, but Nancy deserved the truth. "I'm not a very good lawyer. I could help you find someone else."

"Baloney!" Nancy's face was much too serious for the goofy term I hadn't heard anyone say since my grandma passed away.

I swiped a hand over my lips to wipe the smile away.

"No niece of Stan Dawes could be bad at what she does," Nancy said.

The smile died naturally without my hand's help. In Virginia, I'd had to live with constant comparison to my talented parents. Their firm was the first choice of the wealthy because they got results. I couldn't even speak in front of a jury without ending up tongue-tied.

Part of why I'd come to Fair Haven was to escape that. Instead, I'd apparently jumped from their shadow into Uncle Stan's.

That I-know-you-won't-let-me-down look was back on Nancy's face. Part of what drew me to Fair Haven in the first place was the intense loyalty among Fair Haven residents and the willingness to help each other during times of need.

If I turned her down now, it'd be personal. It'd be like saying I didn't want to help her. Nancy had remained loyal to me and to Sugarwood even when she had to go to the hospital after being accidentally burned. She'd helped me learn how to make maple butter and maple sugar. And she'd stayed up late with me the day of Drew's murder to talk me through making butter tarts so I wouldn't disappoint Mark's parents.

She'd probably received the call from her niece shortly afterward telling her that Drew was dead, Holly was missing, and the police were asking a lot of questions.

"Okay," I said. "I'll do it."

Nancy gave my hand another squeeze and insisted on packaging up most of the goodies on her kitchen table to send home with me as a thank-you.

I slumped back into her too-stiff couch to wait. As hard as I tried to escape being a lawyer, I kept ending up back at this place. This wasn't supposed to be who I was anymore.

If you really wanted to stop, the voice in my head that sounded annoyingly like my mother said, *you wouldn't have gone through the steps to be able to practice law in Michigan.*

The accusation hit a little too close to home.

Chapter 8

The next morning, I put the address that Nancy had given me for her niece's house into my GPS and turned out of the Sugarwood laneway and onto the main road. Nancy had called her niece while I was still at her house the day before and set up an appointment. My parents had taught me that every successful case began with research. If I was going to defend Holly, I needed to know more about her and more about her relationship with Drew. That would prepare me for what kind of case the prosecution would put together in terms of motive. Then I could go about dismantling it.

The thought felt slimy in my brain. It sounded too much like something my parents would think.

I wasn't my parents. If Holly turned out to be guilty, we'd make a plea, just like Nancy said, or I'd have to help her find alternative legal counsel. In the meantime, I'd work on building a case for her defense if she was innocent, including trying to figure out who else might have had a motive to kill Drew. All we needed was reasonable doubt.

My car's GPS took me into a neighborhood of small, tightly packed homes. Most of the driveways were neatly shoveled and salted, but none of them seemed to have much in the way of a yard.

My GPS instructed me to turn right into the next driveway. The older-model red Honda in the driveway matched the description Nancy had given me of her niece's car, and as she'd warned me, the house number was nearly impossible to see from the road because of the porch light. The house itself was weathered white siding and looked like it wouldn't be much bigger inside than the apartment I'd had back in DC.

My stomach felt like it was twisting up. I hadn't talked fees with Nancy yesterday. If the going rates for a quasi-decent defense attorney in Michigan were even close to what they were in DC, it'd cost Nancy more than she earned in a year. And I knew exactly how much she earned in a year because I'm the one who signed off on her salary.

Based on the appearance of her niece's house and my memory of what Drew's mom had said about Drew working hard to save up for Holly's tuition as well as his own, Nancy's niece didn't make more per year than Nancy did.

A woman who looked to be in her early forties stepped out onto the porch, a tan sweater wrapped tightly around her. Her light brown hair was cropped close to her head. She waved.

I left my car and climbed the porch steps. The closer I got, the more Holly's mom reminded me of a faded-out picture.

She extended a hand. Even her handshake felt washed out. "I'm Daisy Northgate. Holly's mom."

Daisy. The bright, cheerful name didn't fit now, but if she'd been anything like Holly in her youth, I could see it fitting once upon a time.

Daisy took my jacket, but didn't hang it up on the set of hooks along the entry way wall. "I think we've wasted your time, and I don't want to take up any more of it. My husband and I discussed it last night, and even with Aunt Nancy's help, we can't afford your services. We'll have to stick with whatever public defender they give Holly."

"There aren't any fees. Your aunt's been kind to me, and I'm glad for the chance to do something nice for her."

The words were out of my mouth before I had a chance to think about them, but as soon as I said them, the tense, twisting feeling in the pit of my stomach evaporated. I couldn't charge them for this. I didn't need the money, and with the maple syrup season coming to an end, I wasn't even needed around Sugarwood right now most of the time. Uncle Stan had clearly been organizing the business to run without him so that he'd be able to retire at some point. Other than the few ideas I had for expanding the business, I was basically superfluous.

Daisy's throat worked and she dipped her head. She hung my coat on the wall.

"How about you show me Holly's room?" I said to save her from having to try to thank me. I could see the thank you. That was plenty for me.

Daisy led me down a narrow hall. It opened up into the small living room and a set of stairs. The whole place felt closed in, a stark contrast to the sunny, open-concept house I'd inherited from Uncle Stan—a house I'd taken for granted as normal because I'd come from similar circumstances.

Daisy started up the stairwell. "The police came with a warrant and took her computer. The rest of her things aren't even the way she left them. Her room was a mess after the break-in we had the other day."

"That's okay. This is just a place for us to start." I'd been so distracted by the trouble I'd caused Erik and Elise and by stepping back into my past life as a lawyer that I'd almost forgotten about the break-in. "Was anything taken?"

Daisy glanced back over her shoulder. "From Holly's room?"

That would be helpful to know, but I also wanted to figure out whether the murder and the break-in were connected. If it'd been kids looking for stuff they could pawn, items should have gone missing from the rest of the house. "From the house in general. Were any electronics missing? Jewelry?"

"They took our computer. It was six or seven years old, so it can't be worth much to them, but it's the only thing we had worth stealing since the police already had Holly's laptop. I don't exactly keep a lot of jewelry or fine china around."

Her gaze skimmed over my white, yellow, and pink gold trinity loop necklace and down to my designer boots.

I smoothed my hands over my skirt. The Milano piqué knit jacket and matching tunic and skirt I'd selected probably cost me more than the Northgates spent on two or three months' rent. When I'd picked it out, I'd only been thinking about appearing professional, and this was one of the outfits I would have chosen to wear to a first meeting with a client back when I worked for my parents' law firm. But their clients easily grossed six, even seven, figures.

To Daisy Northgate, it probably made her feel lesser, judged, maybe even like I wouldn't care about helping her daughter the way I should. I'd have an uphill climb now to prove to her that I cared just as much about Holly as about any of the wealthy clients whose cases I'd worked on. Maybe more, because I believed Holly had a chance at being innocent.

Daisy swung open the door directly at the top of the stairs. "This is Holly's room."

Objectively, the room was tiny, with only a single window on the far wall. Subjectively, it was stunning. Holly had somehow managed to place the furniture and mirrors in such a way that even with both Daisy and I standing in it, it didn't feel cramped. And the flowery greens and purples, colors I never would have thought to put together, added a warmth and vibrancy.

I must have been gawking because Daisy smiled for the first time since she invited me inside. "Holly and Drew fell in love because they were both artists in a way. For Drew, it was photography. For Holly, it was interior design."

The wall I'd accidentally built with my clothing selection seemed to lose a couple bricks.

I moved around the room for a better look. The empty spot on the desk must have been where Holly's laptop normally sat. Papers and photos spread out across her bed. I scooped up a handful. I could immediately tell the ones that had been taken by Drew—his unique viewpoint stood out—but none of them looked important. Most of them were photos that were obviously from Holly's childhood.

But the bed didn't strike me as the place they were usually kept. "Did the police set these out, or were they rummaged through by the intruder?"

Daisy sank down on a clear edge of the bed. It creaked underneath her. "The person who broke in. I think Holly kept them on her desk or in the drawers."

Papers and photos didn't hold value for the average break-and-enter offender. "Only this stuff, or did they go through anything else?"

Daisy did the type of eye roll where her head followed the motion. "They went through everything else. Her clothes were thrown all over the room."

That, though, did sound like a thief scrambling to find anything of value and get out quick. The break-in wasn't the only hint that Holly might not have killed Drew, so even if the two were unconnected, it didn't sign Holly's name into the prison logs.

What night was the fight someone witnessed her having with Drew shortly before the murder.

I cleared a second spot on Holly's bed and wiggled my way up so I could sit with my legs tucked to the side. There wasn't another way to sit on a bed in a skirt and still look even remotely modest. And I doubted Daisy would appreciate a lawyer who seemed like an oaf any more than she'd appreciate a lawyer who wouldn't take their case seriously.

I kept a respectful distance between us and didn't take her hand the way I did Nancy's. Clearly, the lines were going to be different here. What I needed to do was figure out where they were so I could walk them. This would fall apart entirely if Daisy didn't cooperate.

I made sure I caught her gaze before I started. Eye contact, my father used to say, always makes people think you're telling the truth and you're on their side even when you're not. "I'm going to have to ask you some questions you might not like as we work together to protect Holly. Are you ready for that?"

She rested her hand on her chest for a second, like her heart was beating too fast, then nodded her head.

"The police have a witness that claims to have heard Holly and Drew having an argument recently. Do you know what that was about?"

"That." Daisy let out a huff of air and her hand lowered to her side. "They worked that out. Holly told me."

That was completely unhelpful. "I need you to tell me what the argument was about. How did they work it out?"

Her expression turned to granite. She slid off the bed and moved to the far side of the room, her arms crossed over her chest.

And then I understood. She still felt like I'd judge Holly or their family or their life.

I slid to the edge of the bed, but didn't stand up. I didn't want to turn this into a showdown. It couldn't be me against her if we were going to successfully be *us* defending Holly against the accusations leveled at her.

I leaned forward slightly. "I wouldn't normally push for you to tell me things that feel private, but the police will find out everything, even the things you don't want them to. When I go to court with Holly to defend her, I have to know what to expect. I can't protect her otherwise."

"I know." Daisy leaned back against Holly's desk and pinched and released her bottom lip. "I just feel like everything about her will be turned into something bad. Everyone will want to prove she's the kind of person who could kill someone. And she's not. She's not like that."

What must it be like to be a mother who desperately wanted to spare her child from pain and scrutiny but couldn't? I couldn't even begin to guess at all the emotions that must be boiling through her, but anger and frustration were probably high on the list. "I'm going to do my best to make sure that doesn't happen."

She nodded her head, once, twice, like she was internally talking herself into trusting me. "One of Holly's friends saw Drew out to coffee with another girl. The way her friend described it made it sound like Drew was flirting with her and cheating on Holly. Holly..." Her voice took on the throaty quality of someone fighting back tears. "Holly was devastated. She was never the best at choosing the right moment for things, even as a little girl. She screamed at Drew as soon as she tracked him down. Half the town probably saw it."

Based on the evidence Mark shared with me, Holly's impulsivity might actually work in her favor. She didn't sound like the kind of person to carefully plan a murder, and if Drew's assailant was taller than him,

Holly would have had to plan ahead in order to enlist the help of an accomplice.

An accomplice she might have been trying to call on her cell phone right before everyone split up to look for Riley. She'd been intent on catching a signal. Anyone who wasn't a Sugarwood regular wouldn't have known about the spotty reception in the bush and might have thought they could contact their partner with the location.

I pushed the thought aside. My job right now was to assume Holly was innocent until she told me otherwise. And to pray that Nancy was right about Holly's willingness to confess to us if she did do it.

Besides, Holly and Drew seemed to be getting along fine when I saw them. They didn't seem like a couple on the verge of breaking up. "How did Drew explain what Holly's friend saw?"

"He told Holly that he was trying to help the other girl. He'd seen her doing something that could get her in big trouble, and he wanted to warn her. Holly didn't tell me how Drew convinced her of it, but he did."

The urge to smile pulled at my cheeks, and I worked to keep my expression neutral. The fight that seemed to put a big flashing guilty target on Holly actually gave us a lead for who else might have wanted to kill Drew. It could be the other girl, or it could be whoever else was involved in what he saw her doing.

But if that were the case, then one of them had been on the tour with us. Or both of them, since Mark said the murderer was taller than Drew, and none of the women on the tour fit that criterion. "Did Holly tell you who the other girl was?"

Daisy shook her head. "I'm not sure Holly even knew."

It'd been a long shot. At least I knew where to start.

There'd only been one girl on the tour within the right age for Holly's friend to have mistaken their meeting for a date. Even though she wouldn't have been tall enough to stab Drew any more than Holly was tall enough, her father would have been.

Chapter 9

"Did you tell the police what you told me about the argument?" I asked as Daisy walked with me back to the front door.

"They didn't ask." She tugged her sweater tighter around her and kept her arms wrapped around her waist. "Should I have told them?"

The police might not see the source of the argument as a lead the way I did, but they cited the argument itself as a motive for Drew's murder. "It can't hurt. They don't have any other way of knowing Holly and Drew reconciled."

"I'll call today and ask to speak to the officer who questioned me."

I hesitated in the doorway even after I had my coat back on and my keys in my hand. The final thing I needed to do could snap the threads of trust between us. "As Holly's lawyer, it's my duty to encourage her to turn herself in. If you know where she is, now would be the time to tell me."

The corner of her mouth tensed and released as if she were holding back angry words.

If I lost her as an ally now, the chances of getting her back—even with intervention from Nancy—would be slimmer than my chances of becoming coordinated enough to walk a tightrope. *Think like a mom, Nikki. What would convince you to admit to knowing where your daughter was hiding out if you thought you were protecting her by lying about it?*

"It's not even about her turning herself in to the police," I said. "It's still winter. She'd be better off someplace where she can stay warm and fed. And the longer she stays away, the guiltier it makes her look. If she turned herself in, I could use that to bolster our case that she's innocent."

The twitching at the corner of her mouth stopped. "I don't know where she is, but if she calls me, I'll let you know."

I opened the front door and stepped onto the porch. The wind nipped at my legs. The temperature seemed to have dropped again.

My own words spun like gears in my mind, connecting and building on each other. The March weather in

Michigan was still colder than December in Virginia. Holly couldn't be camping, and she'd need to eat. The police would be watching Holly's credit cards for activity. So how was she surviving?

"Did you and your husband check to see if any of your credit cards are missing or if you're shorter on cash than you remember?"

Daisy leaned a hip against the doorjamb, and creases formed a V between her eyes. "We weren't home when someone broke in. We both had our wallets with us. The thief couldn't have taken anything from our wallets."

"I wasn't thinking of the person who broke into your house. Holly might have snuck back in during the night and taken cash or one of your credit cards so she'd have something to live off of that the police wouldn't think to trace."

Daisy grabbed for her purse. It was the most energetic movement I'd seen from her.

She pulled out her credit cards. "There's one missing."

I took the risk and brushed my fingers lightly over her sleeve. "You need to tell the police. If someone breaking into your house wasn't random, they could have been looking for Holly or for something they think she has. She's not safe on her own."

I'd told Russ I wouldn't be back to Sugarwood for the rest of the day, so I might as well spend my time productively and continue looking into Drew's murder now that my participation was official. Holly was somewhere alone, possibly in danger from the real murderer, and if the police couldn't find her, the best way to get her to come back seemed to be to find the real killer. As soon as she saw in the news that someone had been arrested for Drew's murder, she'd have no reason to stay away any longer.

The problem was, where should I start?

My parents always said that you should never ask a question that you didn't already know the answer to. Interrogations should be about confirming your suspicions. Anything else told the person you were questioning what you knew and didn't know. Questions for the purpose of fact-finding gave the upper hand to the opposing side.

Right now, most of the questions I'd ask anyone from the tour would give them the upper hand. If they'd killed Drew, they'd immediately know that I wasn't any closer to finding the real killer than the police were.

The most likely candidate for the real killer seemed to be George Powers. His daughter Amy was the only one on the tour who fit the description of the young woman Holly's friend saw Drew with. That meant I didn't want to start with them. My best option for where to start lay at the other end of the guilt spectrum, with the tourist couple.

Unless one of them was a serial killer—one in seven people was a sociopath, but serial killers are rarer than shows like *Criminal Minds* make them seem—they weren't likely to have killed a man they'd only met that day.

I'd been standing behind the husband at the police station when they made us each turn out our pockets and show our hands, looking for blood on us or our possessions. He'd been carrying one of the old-fashioned keys used by The Sunburnt Arms. After my extended stay there when I first came to Fair Haven for Uncle Stan's funeral, I'd never forget them. The Sunburnt Arms' vintage guest book had even been the inspiration for the guest book I'd set up for tour guests to sign. The idea of having a record of everyone who'd toured our grounds through the years had taken on a nostalgic appeal for me since I'd grown more familiar with the business and how important it was to the community. I imagined putting the guest books into a maple syrup museum one day.

I headed out from the Northgates' and across town to The Sunburnt Arms. The bed-and-breakfast rested on what I'd learned was the affluent side of Fair Haven. The homes and businesses there had the best view of the lake. The Sunburnt Arms booked up for the tourist seasons almost a year in advance, and had belonged to the family of Mandy, the owner, for years. I'd once asked her what she called it to shorten the mouthful of a name since you couldn't exactly go around calling it the TSA. She'd given me the same look that my parents gave to people who tried to call me Nikki rather than Nicole.

Despite that blunder on my part, Mandy was a good friend. I'd found out while staying there that she was an avid mystery reader the same way I was. We'd gotten into the habit of swapping books when we found a new author we loved.

Hopefully, she'd give me the room number of the tourist couple, especially since I couldn't remember whether their last name was Marshall or Martin.

I parked my car in the nearly empty parking lot for The Sunburnt Arms. Either the guests were already out for the day or the off-season slow-down had begun. If the tourist couple wasn't here, my trip would be wasted. Either that or I'd have to camp on Mandy's doorstep until they came back.

The only cars in the lot were Mandy's ancient Toyota, a navy-blue four-door sedan with a baby-on-board sign suction-cupped to the back windshield and Kentucky plates, and a lipstick-red hearse look-a-like SUV with a tiger-striped decal in the shape of a B. The decal was probably for some sports team, but I didn't know which one. The SUV had Ohio plates.

When I asked everyone where they were from at the start of the Sugarwood tour, the tourist couple had said Ohio. The SUV must be theirs. At least the chances seemed good they were in.

I headed up the steps and straight through the front door to the check-in desk.

Mandy perched on her swivel chair, nose deep in a book, as predicted. The rainbow of light from the nearby stained-glass window cast glitters over her naturally silver hair and made her look like Cinderella's fairy godmother come to life—or at least what Cinderella's fairy godmother might have looked like if she were nearly six feet tall, with the build of a lumberjack.

Mandy held up a finger in a be-with-you-in-a-second gesture, then sucked in a sharp breath. She flipped the page, and another half minute passed before she finally looked up.

A smile bloomed on her face. "You have to read this one." She set the book aside, but kept a hand over it like she was afraid I might run off with it before she had a chance to finish. Her gaze slid down my clothing and her face turned a yellow color. "I didn't miss the funeral, did I?"

That sealed it. These clothes were going back in the closet, and I wasn't bringing them out again until I needed to visit my parents. "I had a business meeting."

Mandy cocked her head to one side, reminding me a bit of an eagle about to swoop down and snap up a tasty morsel. In this case, I had the uncomfortable feeling that the tasty morsel was what kind of business I'd been doing that required my big-city-girl clothes.

Mandy saw a conspiracy everywhere. I could almost see her concocting a wild idea that I'd been negotiating the sale of Sugarwood or selling my soul to get Sugarwood syrup into a major chain restaurant.

Thankfully she was only a prawn-sized gossip in the Fair Haven ecosystem. She preferred sharing her theories with close friends rather than spreading them willy-nilly. Last time I'd stopped by, she was convinced that Grant and Mark had switched places for a day just to see if anyone would notice and no one but her had.

"You have a couple staying here," I said before she could prod further, "and I was hoping you'd be able to give me their room number."

"You're not going to try to break in, are you?"

The fact that she even suggested I might spoke to how much work I still had to do on my reputation in this town.

Normally, I could probably tempt Mandy to give up the information by suggesting I was investigating a mystery, but I hadn't gotten Daisy Northgate's permission to share that I'd been hired as Holly's lawyer. Even if I had, I didn't want to set the rumor wheel spinning by sharing that tidbit. As soon as the town found out that Holly's family had hired legal counsel, a thousand crazy stories would pop up about why she'd killed Drew. She'd be convicted in the court of public opinion before she ever made it to trial.

The truth was only going to create more intrigue in Mandy's mind. I'd have to go with a half-truth instead.

I plastered my best hurt look across my face. "I came to offer them either a free Sugarwood tour or a refund of their money. They were part of the tour that got cut short because of what happened to Drew Harris."

"Oh." Mandy peeked at her book like she was wondering how much longer this would take before she could get back to the story world. "Well, I can't give you their room number either way. That would be a breach of privacy laws, I think. I'm not entirely sure, but I'd rather not risk it."

I drooped against the desk. "How about if you called their room and asked if they'd be willing to see me?"

She pinched up her face. "Oh, I don't think I could disturb them that way."

She left me no choice. I'd have to play dirty. Her bookmark sat well past the three-quarter mark, a terrible place to be forced to stop reading anything. I threw an exaggerated glance back over my shoulder at the chairs in the lobby. "If it'd make you feel better, I could pull up a chair and wait for them to come down. I wouldn't mind a little visit with you anyway."

"You know," Mandy reached for the house phone, "I think a phone call would be fine. I wouldn't be telling you anything about them, and they could always tell me they'd prefer not to be disturbed. What did you say the last name was?"

I had a fifty-fifty chance. "Martin?" My intonation added an unintentional question mark.

Mandy's gaze skittered to her book and she gave a
tiny head shake.

"Marshall. Sorry, I meant Marshall."

"I do have a Mr. and Mrs. Marshall. Why don't you
wait over there," she nodded to the far end of the lobby, where I'd have to shout to carry on a conversation
with her, "and I'll check with them."

I gave myself a mental pat on the back.

Less than five minutes later, Mr. Marshall came into
the lobby from the direction of the guest stairs. Now
that his hair was safe from the wind having its way
with it, he wore it in a comb-over that I'd have guessed
was a last attempt at hiding his growing baldness.

He wasn't much taller than me. He was close
enough to Drew's height that I'd have had to see them
standing together to know who was taller. Obviously
that wasn't happening, but if Drew's attacker were
taller than him, Mr. Marshall was definitively off the
list of suspects.

He hesitated in the lobby doorway, and his gaze
swept right over me.

He must not recognize me all dressed up. When I
ran the tour, I bundled up in earmuffs, a scarf, gloves,
and an oversized puffy winter coat that made me look a
little like a purple Pillsbury dough girl.

I rose from my chair and held out my hand. "Mr.
Marshall, I'm Nicole from Sugarwood." I gave him my
best disarming smile. "And yes, I do look a bit different

today. Thank you for agreeing to see me. Will your wife be joining us?"

The narrowing of his eyes was so slight it would have been easy to miss, more of a tightening of the muscles than anything else. "She's resting. I didn't think she needed to be here to discuss a refund for our tour."

His booming voice seemed out of place for his small size, almost like it was trying to compensate for his small stature by being larger than life.

Mandy's gaze was already back on her book, but she hadn't turned a page since Mr. Marshall made his appearance. Eavesdropper. Though perhaps I should be flattered that she hoped this conversation would be more engrossing than her story.

I swept a hand in the direction of the hallway. "Why don't we head back to the breakfast room? It'll be quieter there."

His gaze flickered around the empty lobby. His expression clearly said *quieter than what?* but he followed after me anyway.

We settled into a two-person table to the side of the room closest to where Mandy laid out the breakfast buffet each morning. The smell of sausage and eggs and homemade waffles still hung in the air.

I kept my shoulders back and my posture open. All the lessons my parents had drilled into me over the years about body language cues kicked through my mind at times like this.

First, establish rapport, my mother would say. Get them talking about something non-confrontational.

"You'll see a refund on your credit card statement soon, but I also wanted to offer you a free tour as well. Maybe you can replace the bad memories with some good ones."

Mr. Marshall rested a hand on top of his head and left it there like some sort of vestigial hat. "I appreciate that, but I doubt we'll be taking you up on the offer. My wife has a seizure disorder bad enough she'd not even allowed to drive. Meds don't always help, and stress can trigger 'em. Going out by where that Drew Harris died can't be anything other than stressful."

I could see it now in his eyes and hear it in his voice—the way his lips pushed out the tiniest bit like he was tensing his jaw, the etched circles under his eyes too deep to be made by lack of sleep alone. It all spoke to the toll a chronic illness took on the loved ones involved. Even on the best of days, you constantly watched for the signs that the tide of health was about to turn against you. I'd grown up seeing it in the spouses and children and friends who came with their patient into Uncle Stan's office while I read books in the corner or played with my dolls. I didn't understand what it meant until I got older.

The sides of my chest felt like they'd tipped inward, pressing on my heart. "I'm sorry to hear about your wife's condition. My uncle had a chronic heart condition. It's not easy. On them or on the people who love them."

Good, build that common ground, my mom's voice whispered into my mind.

I wanted to answer back *that's not why I did it,* but talking to yourself was never a good sign.

He lowered his hand. "You understand then how it's not worth the risk." The grin that spread across his face belonged to a guilty little boy rather than a man nearing retirement age. "This is our second honeymoon. We came to Fair Haven for our first, too."

Most of the time, all those things that go wrong in life aren't so terrible in hindsight because they make for funny stories later. I'm pretty sure a time would never come when Mr. and Mrs. Marshall would laugh and say *Hey, remember that time we saw a dead body on our second honeymoon?* I owed them a lot more than a refund and a free tour to make up for that lovely memory, even though Drew's death hadn't been my fault.

Instead of saying all that, though, what I said was, "How long have you been married?"

Because as much as I hated to agree with my mom—in real life or when she was only a figment in my head—she'd been right. The more we shared, the better my chances of him being willing to talk to me about what he might have noticed the day Drew died.

"Seventeen years and then this time a couple of weeks."

This time. My preconceived notions splattered on the floor like a dropped egg.

"I did say it was our second," he said. "We divorced fifteen years ago because I was an idiot. So you can see why I'm not going to let anything take her away from me again."

Before I could answer, Mandy scuttled into the room, bearing a tray with two cups of coffee, a handful of sweeteners, and those little plastic containers of milk and cream. "I thought you two might need some refreshment."

Uh huh. We might like some refreshments and she might like to try to catch a snippet of what we'd been talking about in here so long.

She set a cup down in front of each of us and dropped the additives in the middle of the table, then bustled around by the breakfast bar as if she were cleaning things up. I made some small talk, recommending restaurants and other things the Marshalls might want to do while here.

Finally, Mandy heaved a sigh and left. Maybe at last she'd decided my business here was boring after all and her time would be better spent on that mystery that I just had to read next. I waited an extra minute to be sure I heard her steps shuffle off down the hall.

Mr. Marshall nodded at my cup of coffee. "I notice you're holding it rather than drinking it."

"I've stayed here before."

He held up a hand as if to shield his words in case Mandy reappeared. "My wife claims it cleared her sinuses."

I barely held back an unladylike snort. Mandy wouldn't be getting any five-star reviews based on the quality of her coffee, that was for sure.

Once she finished her book, we might become more interesting than twiddling her thumbs and waiting for the phone to ring. I needed to deal with my actual reason for being here. "I did have one other reason for coming, and it's why I asked if your wife would be joining us. I'm investigating Drew Harris' murder on behalf of a client, and it'd be a great help if you could tell me what you remember from that day."

His eyebrows nearly butted heads above his eyes. "Are you a private investigator as well as working at the maple syrup farm?"

"I'm a lawyer, actually. I've been retained to prepare a defense for the person the police currently believe murdered Drew."

The look that crossed his face was the kind of instinctive flash that people can't always control. Because I don't think he would have wanted to say any of what his look said. It was the *what's a lawyer doing working on a maple syrup farm at all* look. Followed rapidly by the look that I'm pretty sure best translated as *you must be a crappy lawyer if you have to work a second job on the side.*

"Huh," was all he actually said, with a shrug of his shoulders. "Interesting hobby you have."

Since I didn't want to get lost down a rabbit trail, I decided not to launch into the whole story about how I actually co-owned Sugarwood and that being a lawyer, especially a criminal defense attorney, wasn't all sprinkles and unicorn glitter. More often is was worms and rotten tomatoes.

"Could you walk me through what you remember from the tour?" I asked.

"There's not much to tell." He swirled the coffee around in his cup, but didn't risk a sip. "You and Drew came back, and the young couple said their daughter was missing so we all went off to look. We didn't find her, and when we came back to the clearing, almost everyone else was back and he was already dead."

That was about a ten on the unhelpful Richter scale. "Do you think your wife might be able to add anything?"

"I don't see how." His hand was back on the top of his head. "Janet and I were together the whole time because I didn't want her off in the woods by herself, but I can check with her when she wakes up."

Mandy appeared in the door again and held up a plate. "Anyone want a chocolate pastry fresh from the oven?"

I thanked her, took one of the pastries to go—much to her clear chagrin—and slipped Mr. Marshall a Sugarwood business card so he could call me if anything changed.

On the way home, I called Kristen White. She was the next least-likely suspect since she was shorter than Drew and she'd returned with Riley. She wouldn't have had enough time to return to the clearing, kill Drew, and then go back out into the woods to find Riley and bring her back.

"I'm sorry I couldn't be of more help to you or to the police," Kristen said after basically giving me the same *I didn't see anything* spiel I got from Mr. Marshall.

A wail carried through the phone on Kristen's end and filled my car.

"I've got to go," she said, her voice now sounding like she was paying more attention to something in the background than to our conversation. "Do you want me to ask Shawn to call you when he gets home from work?"

"Please."

Before she clicked off the phone, I heard, "Riley, what did I say about hitting your brother?"

Then silence.

The inevitable fights between siblings might have been why my parents stopped with me. I couldn't imagine how they would have reacted to me fighting with a brother or sister.

Children, we don't bicker, I could almost hear my mom saying. *It's not what we do.*

Wait. I smacked my steering wheel. Kristen didn't have their little boy with her when she came back with Riley. That must mean he went with Shawn. That crossed him off the list, too.

Aside from Holly, the only two people remaining without an alibi were George and Amy Powers.

Chapter 10

Trying to hold a Great Dane still enough with one hand to take a picture of her belly incision on my phone with the other hand wasn't as easy as I thought it would be. Why I ever thought it would be easy now escaped me, just like my phone as Velma rolled onto her back and waggled her legs in the air, knocking my phone from my hand and sending it shooting across the floor and under the couch.

I slapped a palm against the floor. I needed to get this picture taken and head off to the Powers' house if I was going to be there in the small window George Powers said they had between when he got home from work and when they had to leave for Amy's swim team practice.

I'd planned to take the pictures of Velma's belly earlier in the day and email them to her vet, but today had ended up being a busier day than expected with Sugarwood business—Nancy wanted me to approve some of the gift basket options she was creating for sale in the Short Stack and on the new website, I'd needed to email some new photographers for rates and availability and tell our website designer we'd hit a delay, and Stacey thought we should upgrade some of our older equipment, a big enough expense that Russ and I both needed to be involved in the decision.

Velma came back upright and raised her "eyebrows" into a quizzical expression as if to say *What? Weren't we playing a game?*

"No game. If you don't let me get this picture, I have to drag you back into the vet to figure out why you're all red." I pressed my palm to my forehead. "And now I'm trying to reason with a dog. You can't even speak English."

I laid flat on my belly and fished around under the couch. Dust and fur coated my hand. Apparently, housekeeping wasn't one of my skills, either, but who knew dogs could shed this much without going completely bald?

My fingertips hit something cold. I wiggled it out. Rubber bone. I tossed it backward over my shoulder for the dogs. The second time I came up with my actual phone.

But now I was definitely out of time.

Can you stop by after work and look at Velma's belly? I texted Mark as I maneuvered Velma and Toby back to their crates.

You know vets and drs go to different schools, right? he wrote back. *Courses on dogs weren't required for my degree.*

I blew a raspberry at my phone. *I just want your quasi-professional opinion on whether I should be worried about her incision.*

Leave the door unlocked. He followed it with a smiley face.

The whole not-locking-the-door thing was still new to me, but I'd been told it wasn't that unusual in small towns or rural communities.

I grabbed my purse and jogged to my car, a little knot in my stomach. Maybe it was my big-city upbringing rearing its suspicious head, but I'd rather get one of those hide-a-key rocks than leave my door unlocked anymore. Nancy had told me that both Daisy and her husband and the Harris' had left their doors unlocked the morning they were robbed. Could it even be *breaking* and entering if your door wasn't locked? Chief McTavish's attempt to help the town by not putting the string of break-ins in the news was probably backfiring. People would go on leaving their doors unlocked like they always had unless the police gave them a reason not to.

But Erik had probably had the same thought. I'd have to let him handle it. Me leaving even a friendly suggestion would only put another black mark beside my name in Chief McTavish's mental book.

I pulled into the Powers' driveway at the same time as Amy came up the sidewalk with a Golden Labrador. Based on the mud part way up his legs, they were probably coming back from the dog park I'd seen on my way into their neighborhood.

She watched me climb out of the car and her face sagged. She stroked her fingers over the top of the dog's neck and straightened her back in a gesture that looked like a person bracing themselves to hear they needed yet another surgery or round of chemo. She hurried forward.

When she stopped next to me, the dog dropped into an immediate sit. A little worm tendril of envy ate at the core of my heart after my battle of wills with Velma. Not that I'd ever trade Velma even for the best trained dog in the universe, but it would be nice when we got through the stage where she challenged me on everything.

"I know we forgot to come back to pay for our tour," Amy said before I could even greet her. "We weren't trying to not pay. I've been thinking about it since you called my dad last night. Maybe I could do some work for you at Sugarwood to make up for it."

Before I'd called George Powers, I'd decided to use the same let-me-make-up-for-the-awful-tour-experience ploy as I used with Mr. Marshall to gain entrance. Except all I'd said on the phone was that I wanted to talk about the tour.

Clearly they'd assumed I was coming to demand payment.

The fact that she'd thought it through at all told me a lot. The money troubles that resulted in their credit card being declined weren't recent, they weren't going away any time soon, and she was willing to do what she could to help her dad. All of that fit with the idea that she'd been engaging in something illegal to ease their financial issues and Drew spotted her. She might even be the one breaking into homes around Fair Haven.

If their problems were that desperate, it wasn't outside the realm of possibility that Amy told her dad what she'd been doing and that Drew knew, too. Her dad might have felt that the only way to keep Drew from exposing Amy's activities and causing them more problems was to kill him.

Hopefully, if their problems were that advanced, I'd also be able to suss them out by poking around their home a little.

"Or maybe we could work out a payment plan." Amy clamped her bottom lip between her teeth. "I know the tickets don't cost much, and it probably seems like we should be able to pay it right away, but things are a little tight right now."

My parents had been emotionally unavailable and hard to please, but one thing I could say for them was that I'd always felt safe—financially and physically.

Maybe too much so, since when I told Mark I'd taken Holly's case, he accused me of thinking I was invulnerable.

"Don't worry about that," I said. "I'm not here to insist you pay."

She gave me a wide-eyed *uh huh* look but led me inside. "Dad? I'm home, and Nicole Dawes is here."

George Powers came down the stairs. His clothes hung on him in a way that said they'd fit him better when he bought them. His skin seemed almost translucent, like wet paper.

He led me into a comfortable living room with furniture that was broken in but not old.

Once we were seated, Amy brought us each a glass of water. Without being asked. Maybe she was too young to think about asking a guest if they'd like anything. Maybe she was hoping to keep my visit as short as possible and coffee would have taken time. Or maybe they didn't have anything else in the house to serve me.

My heart suddenly felt heavy and stiff. Each beat hurt a little. Whoever killed Drew should receive justice, but murder was never that simple. George Powers might not be a bad person. He might simply be a desperate one. A desperate one with a daughter who clearly cared about him as much as Drew and Holly's families cared about them.

That feeling in my heart—maybe it was why my parents were the way they were. They couldn't spend their lives working in the court system, where there weren't ever any real winners, and continue to care. Their hearts would have stiffened until they shattered.

George Powers cleared his throat. He and Amy were staring at me.

Great. How long had I been sitting there without saying anything? They must think I had some sort of disorder. Then again, that couldn't hurt in this case. I didn't want them suspecting yet that I was there for any other reason than to talk about the tour.

"I'm think we've had a bit of a misunderstanding." My voice cracked, and I took a gulp of the water. "I'm not here to demand payment for your tour. I'm here to offer you a free tour to make up for how the one you booked ended up."

George reached for his glass of water. His hand shook slightly as he brought the glass to his lips.

A drug addiction, perhaps? That would explain his weight loss and sickly appearance. A drug addiction would also explain their money problems, and if anyone found out, it could mean jail time. If he and Amy's mom weren't together anymore, it could also mean losing custody of his daughter.

Drew wanted to be a photojournalist, so he might have been investigating drug use in Fair Haven, assuming if he broke a big story it could be a way to bypass college and get a job right away.

George looked back at Amy where she stood behind him on the other side of the couch. "What do you think, sweetie? Did you want to go back?" He swiveled around to face me again, and the gallows expression he'd worn before had lightened. "The tour was her birthday present. She loves everything sweet, and we've lived here all of Amy's life without ever touring Sugarwood."

Amy open her mouth, but closed it without saying anything. She nodded her head, but her arms crossed over her chest like she was closing herself off, afraid I'd pull the offer away.

My instincts told me not to push for anything more today. It'd taken longer to get them to start relaxing with me than it had taken Mr. Marshall. If I poked around the edges of what had happened to Drew today, my training said they'd know what I was doing and close ranks.

The next time, I needed to find a way to talk to Amy alone. The problem was how to do that in a way that wouldn't make her suspicious. Based on what I'd seen, if she realized I was investigating her father, I'd get nowhere.

Now, though, wasn't the time to mull over options. Before I left, I still wanted to get a peek at more of their house to see if I could spot anything that might give me additional information.

I stood. "Give me a call and let me know what day works for you. I'll set it up. Would you mind if I used your bathroom before I go?"

"It's upstairs," George said. "We only have the one."

He half rose to his feet, but Amy dropped a hand on his shoulder. "I'll show her."

I trailed her up the stairs. Family pictures lined the wall that showed Amy, George, and a black woman with thick hair and a beautiful smile. That must be Amy's mom. Even though Amy inherited her dad's lighter skin tone, I could see her mom in her high cheekbones, curly hair, and brown eyes. She'd probably have her smile too, but I hadn't seen Amy smile since I arrived.

The woman in the photo hadn't been with them on the tour, and there weren't any other signs of her around the house, like a coat or shoes. The automatic assumption would be that she left because of the drug problem, but what kind of a mother would leave her daughter behind in that kind of situation? Besides, I'd learned from my mistake with Mark that a person could as easily be a widower. Amy's mom could also be dead.

"Your mom is really pretty," I said.

Amy didn't turn around or look back. "Yeah, she was."

Past tense. So she'd passed. She hadn't left due to some issue in the marriage. Strike that theory off the list.

Amy pointed at a door partway down the hall.

I ducked into the bathroom and closed the door. It was a jack-and-jill, with access to the rooms on either side. I eased one of the adjoining doors open. It creaked and I flinched. Hopefully Amy had gone back down-stairs. I edged into the room.

Based on the dark brown comforter on the bed and the bare walls, the room likely belonged to George, not Amy. My feet seemed to stick to the carpet. Each step got more difficult as I moved into the room.

I couldn't do this. It felt wrong and invasive. I wasn't a police officer. I couldn't in good conscience rifle through their dresser drawers. If it turned out George Powers hadn't done it, I'd have snooped around where I definitely didn't belong.

I backed up into the bathroom, and closed the door again as quietly as possible.

To keep this from being a complete waste, I could take a look in their medicine cabinet. Everyone did that, right? I'm sure I'd read a statistic somewhere that forty percent of people snooped around while in other people's bathrooms.

The cabinet door opened quietly, thank goodness. If everything had fallen out into the sink and made a hid-eous crash, even I couldn't come up with a reasonable explanation.

The contents looked pretty unexceptional. Aspirin, dental floss, q-tips and tweezers, tampons, some laxa-tive, anti-nausea tablets, and a few prescription medi-cine bottles.

One prescription belonged to Amy. Amoxicillin that had expired a year ago. Amoxicillin was the antibiotic I'd taken when I had my wisdom teeth out. There wasn't anything abnormal about it. A couple of pills remained in the bottle. Someone really should have made sure she took them all, but they clearly had bigger things to think about.

The other bottle belonged to George. Oxycodone— a highly addictive opiod painkiller. The prescription was fairly recent, only about a month ago, but the bottle was completely empty.

I'd been looking for evidence of a drug addiction, and I might have found it.

Chapter 11

I swung by Dad's Hardware Store on my way home. I was standing in the aisle, trying to decide whether a plastic lawn bunny or a rock that looked nothing like a real rock would be the least obvious for hiding a spare key, when my phone rang. Mark.

I swiped my finger across the screen to answer.

"I didn't like the look of her incision, so I called the vet's office, and they suggested I email a picture. She's been wearing her cone the whole time, right?"

"I've even made her sleep with it." I selected a rock that I might be able to disguise with a few strategically placed leaves and headed for the locksmith desk to pick up the new copy of my key. The implication of Mark's words finally sunk in. "Wait, you got a picture of her belly?"

"Yeah. I'm surprised you didn't think of it."

That scoundrel dog. Was it worse to have Mark think I'd missed an obvious solution or to confirm that I apparently couldn't control my own dog as well as someone who wasn't her owner? He already knew I was the clumsiest person imaginable, so I might as well keep his respect for my intelligence. "I did. She wasn't having it."

Mark chuckled. "Children are always worse for their parents, I've heard. The vet said that if she wasn't licking it, then she must have an allergy to the sutures. If you go by before they close, they'll have some cream you can put on it until the stiches dissolve. And she needs to stay as quiet as possible until the swelling goes down."

After I paid for my key and pseudo-rock, I headed toward the veterinarian's office instead of going home the way I'd planned. Mark stayed on the call with me as it switched from my phone to my car.

Velma had already been going stir-crazy, being limited to a single long walk a day. Restricting her even more wasn't going to be fun for any of us. "I've already been having trouble keeping her and Toby from playing in the house. Hopefully the cream speeds things up."

"Why don't you take him to a dog park? He could play with other dogs there and maybe it'd be easier to keep them both quiet."

Amy had been coming home from the dog park near their house when I pulled up. Mark had given me my answer to how to talk to Amy alone in a way that wouldn't make her suspicious.

I almost told Mark he was brilliant, but I knew how he felt about me taking part in another investigation.

Tomorrow, Toby and I would head to the dog park.

On Saturday morning, I pulled into the gravel parking strip alongside the dog park for the third day in a row. Amy Powers and her dog hadn't shown up on Thursday or Friday afternoon.

Before I even stopped the car, Toby's thick tail beat against the back seat. If nothing else, he'd enjoyed being able to run and play again, but if Amy didn't show up today, I might have to give up and pursue another plan. Every day Nancy asked me if there'd been any progress. Daisy wasn't sleeping, and Nancy told me that Holly's father was on the verge of losing his job because he'd been spending all his time searching for Holly, terrified that someone had killed her as well.

We went in through the gate, and I let Toby off his leash. I took a seat on the cool bench. Maybe I'd already spent too much time hoping Amy would show up. I didn't even have any proof she came every day or even once a week. I'd hoped, since their house didn't have much in the way of a backyard.

A golden streak blitzed past me.

"Nicole?" a familiar young female voice said from behind me. "What are you doing here?"

Prayer answered. I smiled back over my shoulder at Amy. "I spotted the park when I visited your house and decided to bring my dog."

Amy held back from the bench and wound her dog's leash through her fingers. "Can't you just let him run free around Sugarwood?"

Drat. I hadn't expected to need an explanation for coming here. Toby's presence should have been enough. "My other dog was spayed about a week ago and he's bored without someone to play with." That I-can't-decide-if-you're-lying-to-me-look was still on her face. "And...if I just let him run around where she could see him, I thought she'd be jealous."

I would have thunked my own forehead if that wouldn't have given my lie away.

Amy lowered onto the bench next to me. "Makes sense."

Who would have thought it? She must have figured no one would come up with that silly a lie. If I'd come up with anything better, it might have actually set off her BS detector.

She planted her elbows on her knees but didn't pull out her phone the way I'd expected.

Finally I'd caught a break. That should make a conversation easier to start.

"I didn't thank you properly," Amy said without looking at me.

Or maybe I'd let her lead and I'd follow and wait for an opening.

"You made my dad really happy, and that means a lot." She picked at the cuticle on her thumb. Her nails were chewed down so that none of the white remained. "He felt like he'd let me down because that was what I wanted to do together for my birthday and we couldn't afford to pay for another tour."

For some reason, even with my mom's voice in my head telling me I was a fool, the honest approach seemed like the right way to go. Maybe it was because Amy's expression suddenly looked like fine china teetering on a table edge.

"I noticed your dad didn't look well when I was at your house this week," I said softly.

"Cancer." The word sounded like a punch, like she wanted to attack something but there wasn't really anything she could fight against.

I felt the blow in my stomach nonetheless. Cancer explained his weight loss and frail appearance. And the anti-nausea meds I'd seen in their medicine chest. Many cancer treatments made patients sick to their stomachs.

It explained the Oxy, too. Depending on what type of cancer he had, he could be in a lot of pain.

It even explained the financial troubles. Most health insurance only covered a certain percentage of medical bills and had limits. If he'd had a prolonged battle, the co-pay could have added up, and they might even have exceeded their coverage.

Amy was carrying the burden of all that alongside her dad, after having already lost her mom.

My heart felt like it sank down until I was sitting on it. I didn't want to keep poking into their life. I didn't want to know what she might have been doing wrong. If George Powers had cancer, he might not have even had the strength to stab Drew, so continuing to investigate could lead nowhere. And yet I had an obligation to Holly and Nancy and Daisy, too.

Amy looked up at me from her hunched-over position, reminding me a bit of Drew's mom when she came to my door, just needing someone to lean on for a few minutes.

Regardless of what trouble she might have gotten herself into, she was still a person who was hurting. If Amy didn't have a grandma or an aunt she was close to, it might have been a long time since she'd had anyone offer her the kind of hug that said *it's going to be okay*.

I held out my arms and Amy fell into them.

Screw my parents' ideas of right and wrong and how to handle suspects. They thought my ability to get people to open up to me was some kind of superpower. It was the one thing they'd seemed to respect about me.

It wasn't a superpower. It was that I cared about people, and they sensed it. The ironic part was that my parents saw that caring as a flaw. So the thing they valued about me most was made possible by the thing they wanted to break me of.

Amy's body shook against my shoulder, and I rubbed her back. She pulled herself together quickly, like she was used to having to let her emotions out in a quick burst and then hide them again. She probably was. She wouldn't want her dad to know how hard this was on her and only let herself cry in the shower or when she came to the dog park with their dog and no one else was looking.

She swiped under her eyes with the edge of her sleeve, pushed out by her thumb. "You were a lawyer, right? Before you came here."

If my head hadn't been attached to my shoulders, she would have set it spinning with the topic change. "I'm still a lawyer, yes."

"If you get caught doing something that's technically wrong, but you're doing it for a good reason, do juries go easier on you? Like maybe let you off with community service or something." She was back to avoiding my gaze.

My chest felt like it was trying to split down the middle. Now that I didn't want to keep pushing, she was going to tell me what she'd done, and if it pointed to her or her dad being guilty of Drew's murder, I'd have to use it against her, betraying her trust.

But I was in too deep to back out and betray the trust Nancy placed in me. I gave Amy the space she seemed to need in order to talk about this by watching Toby sniff and paw at the grass forty feet away.

"It depends on the crime," I said.

"Not anything that hurt anyone." Her face snapped in my direction again. "Hypothetically of course. That means I'm just asking about a situation out of curiosity and not that I'm saying I did anything. I've seen that on TV."

The girl was too sharp for a seventeen-year-old. I didn't know what she wanted to do when she finished high school, but she'd make a good police officer or lawyer.

I nodded. "Of course. What were you thinking of? Hypothetically."

She went back to examining her cuticles. "Like if a person couldn't afford expensive prescription pain killers, but someone they really loved was suffering, and so they wanted to try to buy them from a drug dealer instead. If they got caught, and it was their first time getting in trouble, and they told the court why they did it, would they still have to go to jail?"

Double holy crap. That must be what Drew saw her doing. Or trying to do. But she'd said *not anything that hurt anyone.* And the tense she'd used in her question sounded like she hadn't actually bought any drugs yet, which meant neither she nor her dad would have any reason to hurt Drew.

But it was time now to stop the hypothetical. I had to get some solid answers from her, and then I had to make sure she didn't go through with buying drugs from a dealer. Despite what she seemed to think, dealers' product didn't tend to be less expensive unless it was cut with something. And if they convinced her to take product on credit and she couldn't pay it back, the way they'd extract payment could ruin her whole life.

I shifted on the bench so I was angled toward her. "Are you hoping I'll tell you something different from what Drew said?"

Her face turned so red it was nearly purple. "You know about that?"

"I know that Drew caught you doing something illegal and tried to warn you to stop."

Amy dug the toe of her boot into the muddy ground. "I wasn't actually doing anything illegal yet, but Drew saw me waiting for the dealer and he somehow knew what I was planning. He made me go with him to get a cup of coffee to talk about it. He was a senior on the boys' swim team when I was a freshman, and he helped me improve my times. He knows—knew about my scholarship to college and said if I got busted, I'd lose it."

Holly's friend must have seen them having coffee together. Drew's attempts to convince her to stop trying to buy drugs could have easily been misinterpreted by someone walking by. "He was right. And I don't think your dad would want drugs you'd gotten illegally."

She shrugged with that practiced nonchalance that teenagers seemed to have a market on.

Drew's presence at her meeting place couldn't have been coincidence. Perhaps I hadn't been entirely wrong in my theory that he'd been trying to break a story. If he'd been working on a story about a local drug dealer, that could have easily gotten him killed.

I didn't know how they'd managed to kill him with my tour group around without anyone spotting them, but it was my best lead at the moment. It might turn out to be what broke the case if Amy could identify the person she was supposed to meet.

"I'm not going to tell anyone that you were trying to buy drugs, but I do need you to tell me more about it. It might help me figure out why someone would have killed Drew. How did you learn about where to get drugs?"

Amy picked at her fingernail, and a bead of blood appeared. She sucked it away. "I overheard a couple kids at school talking about getting high over the weekend. I asked them where I could get some. They gave me a phone number I was supposed to text with this weird string of numbers and letters. It was like a code so he'd know you weren't a cop."

The dealer was smart, meaning it was possible he'd come up with a way to kill Drew in the midst of all of us. He was also going to be hard to identify if Amy didn't know who he was. He no doubt hadn't listed his phone number under his real name. "So when you sent the code, he sent you a time and place to meet?"

"Yeah, and he said to bring cash."

Then Drew showed up at that same spot and foiled the deal. "Do you have any idea who you were texting?"

She shook her head. She chewed at her nail bed again like she couldn't help herself. Maybe she couldn't. There was only so much stress a human psyche could hold inside before it had to vent somewhere.

"I think he must have seen me with Drew," she said, "that day of the original meet-up, because it seemed like he didn't trust me anymore after. When I tried to set up another meeting, the texts said I needed to send my schedule and they'd find me."

My muscles knotted into little balls under my shoulder blades, sending lines of tension up into my neck. If Amy told him she'd be on the Sugarwood tour and the dealer tried to meet her there, only to see Drew again, he could have thought it was a setup. That would be reason enough to kill Drew.

"Did you text him your schedule the day of the tour?"

Amy did a single shoulder shrug. "Yeah, but he never showed."

I wasn't about to tell Amy that her text might have been a domino in the line that eventually got Drew killed. She couldn't have anticipated the results of her actions, and she certainly didn't need that extra weight to haul around.

At least I knew what to investigate next.

But before I left her and her dad alone, there was one thing we still needed to settle, because she'd admitted that even after Drew warned her away and gave her good reason for it, she'd still tried to contact the dealer again.

I got to my feet and called to Toby. "Please call your dog. I'm going to meet you at your house."

Amy's hand sagged down from her mouth but stayed suspended in mid-air. "You're not going to tell my dad, are you? Because I'll deny it."

I rolled my eyes and made sure she saw it. "I'm not going to tell him. I'm going to take you to the pharmacy, fill your dad's prescription, and leave my credit card on file, with instructions for them to charge it whenever he needs his medication refilled."

The half-scared, all-ego look on her face told me she was considering saying something about how they couldn't let me do that, that they'd manage. But the way her lips twitched like she was holding back tears again also told me how bad she wanted to accept.

I pointed a finger at her and gave her my best grown-up stare. "If you argue with me, I'll tell your dad everything you told me today. I have a feeling you know as well as I do that he'll believe it."

Chapter 12

Over dinner at A Salt & Battery, I confessed to Mark how I'd spent my day and flashed him my best don't-be-mad smile. "I don't know how to pass the information on to Chief McTavish, but I feel like I should."

I munched another "chip" from the plate of my favorite fish and chip dinner. The restaurant was so busy tonight that we'd had to wait nearly twenty minutes for a table.

Mark rubbed the space between his eyebrows with his pointer and middle finger. "It's going to be Alderaan versus the Death Star when he finds out you're investigating this."

Lovely. "I don't suppose I'm the Death Star in that analogy."

Mark's dimple peeked out seemingly against his will. It vanished equally as fast. "You do need to tell him, though. It'll be safer for the police to conduct the rest of the investigation."

I added *overprotective* to my mental list of Mark's major flaws, right after *jealous*.

After I told my mom that Mark and I were dating, the only thing she'd said other than "a doctor is a good choice" was that I should make note of all Mark's flaws so I'd be going into any commitment with all the facts. Then if we got married, I should only pay attention to his strengths and good qualities from that point on. Essentially, my mom's recipe for a happy marriage was *go in with your eyes open and then close them.*

In hindsight, that explained a lot about how my parents, both competitive high-achievers with questionable ideas about morality, had stayed happily married for nearly thirty-five years.

"He's going to feel like I intentionally found a way to circumvent his orders. He already thinks I'm a menace."

"Does it matter what he thinks?"

Aside from the fact that I wanted everyone to like me, it shouldn't have mattered. *Shouldn't have* being the key part of that phrase. "I guess not, but as a lawyer, having a good working relationship with the police doesn't hurt."

My parents' relationship with police had always been confrontational. Perhaps that was unavoidable as a defense attorney.

Mark's eyebrow shot up into a facial question mark. "I thought you didn't want to be a lawyer."

I didn't want to be a defense attorney like my parents, and I didn't want to practice the kind of law Tom McClanahan practiced, spending his days writing wills and contracts and dealing with property sales. And prosecuting attorneys had to make their case in court. My public speaking skills weren't going to magically improve after all these years.

I jammed an oversized bite of fish into my mouth. Directly across from me, a uniformed officer came through the front door, shaking snow off his jacket. Shortly after I dropped Amy back off at home, winter had decided it wasn't going to go quietly.

The officer took his hat off, revealing a shock of red hair.

"Speak of the..." I couldn't really call an officer of the law a devil.

Mark looked back over his shoulder and raised a hand in greeting. Chief McTavish nodded in return and headed for the take-out counter to our left. That effectively put an end to our conversation, at least until he left, and for longer if I could help it. I wasn't entirely sure how to answer Mark's question.

"Nicole!" Mr. Marshall's booming voice carried over the sounds of conversation and silverware clinking against plates. Janet Marshall was at his side this time.

They stopped beside our table. "We can't thank you enough for the recommendation of this place. How's the investigation going?"

At the edge of my vision, I caught a sharp movement from where Chief McTavish waited for his order. I forced myself not to look over even though the need to turn pressed on me more than the desire to scratch an itch that was just out of reach. Even I wasn't enough of an optimist to hope he hadn't heard Mr. Marshall's question. Everyone at the nearby tables must have heard. Turning to look at the chief would only confirm my guilt and potentially make it seem like I was flouting my disobedience. If I ignored him, maybe he'd think they were asking about something else I was looking in to. Some Sugarwood business.

And tomorrow we'd get word that flying pigs had replaced the reindeer for Santa's sleigh.

I'd keep my answer vague and hope with the noise Chief McTavish couldn't catch every word. "It's progressing."

"Say again?" Mr. Marshall tapped a hand to his ear. "Janet keeps telling me I should get my hearing tested. Normally I hear fine, but tonight might have convinced me."

"It's progressing." I cleared my throat and rolled my lips together. Must stop this conversation. "I can't really share anymore."

"Of course not." Janet Marshall spoke for the first time. She leaned against her husband, her arm tucked through his. "We wouldn't expect you to. I just wanted to come over because Ted said you were hoping we'd seen something that would help you with your case. But there's nothing I can add that he didn't already tell you. I wanted to make sure you knew since we're leaving on Thursday."

"Heading home?" Mark asked.

Mr. Marshall shook his head. "This trip hasn't turned out how we planned, so we've decided to extend our honeymoon and go someplace warmer and more relaxing for Janet, like the Maldives. Nostalgia was a nice idea, but it's time we visited some white sandy beaches."

I thanked them and wished them well, and they headed off. I couldn't tell for sure if Chief McTavish still stood at the counter or not, but the hairs on the back of my neck insisted he was there. Still there and glowering at me. My heart did its best imitation of a moth bouncing against a window pane. If he were still there, he'd probably heard all of that. He'd know I was investigating the case he'd specifically told me to stay out of.

I caught Mark's gaze and mouthed the words *Is Chief McTavish still there?*

A cell phone rang from the direction of the take-out counter. "McTavish," the chief's voice said.

That answered my question. I risked a glance over. He was now focused on whatever the person on the other end of the phone was saying.

He swore. "On my way."

He snatched up his Styrofoam food containers and leveled a glare in my direction that looked a lot like the one parents gave to their children when they misbehaved out in public. The one that said "this isn't over."

As soon as he was gone, I pushed my plate away, crossed my arms on the table top, and planted my chin in the crook. "I bet if he decides to 'take care of me,' they'll never find my body."

Mark simply shook his head tolerantly. "Now you're being melodramatic. He'd never kill you. Lock you in a cell, maybe, but not kill you."

I stuck my tongue out at him. "How comforting."

My phone vibrated in my purse. Normally I wouldn't have answered it when Mark and I were out to dinner, but he was signaling the waitress for our check.

I opened my purse and wiggled the phone around. At least I could check who was calling.

The display read Daisy Northgate.

Dread slithered down my back, leaving a cold trail, and Chief McTavish's reaction to the phone call he'd received flashed through my mind.

My voice seemed broken. It refused to work on my first try to answer.

"Nicole Fitzhenry-Dawes," I finally squeaked out.

"My husband found Holly." Daisy's voice was thick, and not with happy tears. "The hospital already called the police. We need you right away."

Mark drove me straight to the hospital. He offered to come up with me, but I asked him to wait downstairs, where he'd be safe from the fallout of Chief McTavish. Just because he couldn't order me to stay away from the case anymore didn't mean he wouldn't make life difficult for anyone he suspected of aiding me.

Daisy had texted me the floor to meet her on. If I remembered the layout of the hospital—and I should, given how many times I'd been there recently—it wasn't a floor with long-term rooms. That meant they either planned to release her today or she was still being treated and hadn't yet been moved. Based on how frantic Daisy sounded on the phone, I'd guess the latter.

The elevator doors opened, and I didn't have to look for the right place. Daisy and her husband stood next to the nurse's station counter with Chief McTavish.

His eyes bugged out of his head like a classic cartoon character, but he strode toward me with the dignity I would have expected from an experienced officer.

As much as I hated to admit it, I had to admire his self-control.

He said something to the Northgates as he passed them and intercepted me before I could get close to them. "I tried to be nice about this, Miss. Fitzhenry-Dawes, but now I'm going to need to be firm. Unless you stay away from my investigation of the death of Drew Harris, I'll be forced to charge you with obstruction."

It was an idle threat. I hadn't done anything to obstruct the investigation, nor was there anything criminal about talking to people. I hadn't tried to influence their statements or taint the evidence in any way.

Had I been a normal person who didn't know his threat was as solid as a leaky balloon, I might have been scared away, though.

Instead, I took off my mitts and stuffed them into my pocket—letting my body language indicate my intention to stay before my words. "As Holly Northgate's legal counsel, I have every right to be here if you intend to question her."

His facial expression didn't even twitch. Not the corner of his eye. Not the edge of one lip. The man was better than even I'd given him credit for.

He stepped aside and swung his arm in an arch indicating I should precede him.

Daisy left her husband's side and met me halfway there. And wrapped me in a hug.

My arms dangled trapped at my sides, and all the professional things I'd planned to say dripped right out my ear.

Daisy released me quickly. "It's thanks to your idea about the credit card that we found her. I told the police like you said, but I watched my statements, too. We saw a charge near where one of Holly's old high school friends lived. The police had already checked with all her friends, but no one searched their parents' outbuildings. My husband went to their door and asked if he could look in the little shed where they keep their gardening supplies, and there she was. When she didn't wake up, he picked her up and brought her here."

Her husband had the muscles of someone who did physical labor for a living. When she said he *picked her up*, I had a feeling it was literal.

I couldn't stop myself from sliding a glance in Chief McTavish's direction. He seemed to be listening. Hopefully he'd heard that I told the Northgates to tell the police about the missing credit card.

But it was time to start laying the professional groundwork between us. "No one's spoken with her yet, have they?"

Daisy waved her husband forward. "We're still waiting for the doctors to give us an update on whether she's awake and going to be okay."

"They said it was a good thing I found her when I did," Mr. Northgate said.

His voice reminded me a bit of Morgan Freeman's. He could have been a voice actor in a different world.

"I'm happy to wait with you if you want until she wakes up."

Daisy and her husband exchanged an in-over-their-heads glance.

"Does she need to have a lawyer with her at all times once she's awake?" Daisy asked.

"Not at all." I modulated my voice into my best imitation of my mom's take-charge tone. "But no one should ask her any questions about the case without me present. Not even you, okay? If the police want to talk to her, for any reason, I need to be there."

It was my parents' rule. If the police wanted to talk one of their clients, all they got was name, rank, and serial number—metaphorically speaking—unless they had legal counsel present.

Since this was my first time flying solo on a case I might actually have to argue, their operating procedures seemed like a decent place to start. I'd modify them as I went along to make them something that wouldn't cost me sleep at night as well.

Since we had no word on how long it might be before the doctors allowed anyone to see Holly, the Northgates decided they didn't need me to stay. Daisy promised to call me as soon as they knew anything.

Chief McTavish walked with me silently back to the elevator and pressed the down button. When the doors opened, I stepped inside. He didn't.

The doors started to close, and he leaned forward slightly and blocked them with one hand. "I'll be checking up on you. For those people's sake, I hope that you are what you say you are."

"What do you think he meant by that?" I asked Mark for at least the third time as we drove back to my house after church the next day. "He made it sound like he thinks I'm only pretending to be a lawyer."

"He probably does think that. You did say the first time he talked to you he treated you like someone with a fetish."

When he'd warned me away, he had admitted to suspecting I'd committed the crimes in order to get the glory of solving them. Given that was his initial profile of me, it made sense he'd now think I might be pretending to be a lawyer to insert myself into a case I'd been prohibited from joining.

"Not a flattering picture," I said.

Mark chuckled. "At least he's not the type to join in the game of telephone this town plays with every hint of a rumor."

I spread my hands apart in the air, mimicking a billboard. "Breaking news: Lawyer and maple syrup maven arrested as criminal mastermind behind all crimes committed in Fair Haven for the past thirty years."

"Maybe not thirty years. Even the Fair Haven rumor mill couldn't suspect you of committing crimes as an infant."

Mark parked his car in front of my house, and we headed up the walkway. As much as The Burnt Toast's Sunday brunch was calling my name, my waist was yelling louder that we needed to stay in and eat a salad today. I'd even grilled the chicken ahead of time last night so I would have a strong motivation not to talk myself out of it.

The red flag on my mailbox was up. That was weird. A lot of things were different here from back in DC, but mail delivery wasn't one of them. Nothing should have come on a Sunday. It could be a flyer for some event, but I didn't want to risk that Stacey had left me something she wanted me to look over. Getting her to take a day off was becoming increasingly challenging. I was close to sic'ing her parents on her.

I tossed Mark my keys. "Can you let the dogs out of their crates?"

My throw went wide, whizzed by Mark's face, and landed somewhere in the remains of the flower bed.

I scrunched up my face and headed for the mailbox, trying to ignore that my internal heater had suddenly cranked the temperature to the point where I'd need to take my coat off to be comfortable. At least Mark had known about my clumsiness before we started dating.

I dropped the flag and pulled the single envelop from the box. It didn't have my name or address on it, so it probably was from Stacey.

Now that my blush had died down, the air felt twice as cold. I scurried into the house after Mark, popping open the envelope as I went. Whoever sent it hadn't sealed it.

Mark already had Velma and Toby out, and Velma lay sedately on her side while he scratched under the edge of her collar and examined her belly. Traitor.

Mark stopping scratching, and Velma rolled to her feet in a move that seemed like it should be too fast and coordinated for a dog her size. She reached me in two bounds and leaned against my leg.

Mark brushed off his knees. "The cream doesn't seem to be helping."

"Good to know I wasn't imagining it."

I tugged the single sheet of paper from the envelope and unfolded it.

The message was handwritten. *Please stop investigating. You're going to send a good person to prison for murdering a bad one, and you don't want to end up like Drew Harris.*

Chapter 13

The first thought that entered my head shot straight to my lips. "What kind of a criminal handwrites a note?"

Mark looked like I'd slapped him in the face. "I hope that's a rhetorical question."

I waved the sheet of paper in his direction. "Someone wants me to stop investigating Drew's death." The room swayed a touch, like I was standing on the deck of a boat rather than on solid ground. "Someone who knows where I live."

Mark's expression changed while I was talking. Now I saw what the people he worked with must see—a capable professional. His gaze focused on the letter, and creases built into a wall on his forehead. "Hold it up for me so I can read it."

I did as he asked.

"Looks like we were right to think Holly didn't kill Drew," he said. "She certainly didn't write the note, and given how desperate her parents have been to find her and have her defended, I can't see them writing it, either."

I gingerly folded the paper back up, trying to only touch places I'd already touched, and tucked it back into the envelop. Maybe if the sender was foolish enough to write it by hand, they'd also neglected to wear gloves.

Mark must have had the same thought, because he took both dogs by the collars and led them off to their room.

I slid my coat back on. As unsettling as it was to think a murderer knew where I lived—again—it meant I'd done something to make them nervous enough to hope a warning would keep me from investigating further.

Shivers ran down my skin like I'd fallen into an ant colony. All this note really proved was that someone didn't want me investigating.

The person who seemed most opposed to my involvement right now was the same person we were about to take the note to.

Mark returned, and I took a step back away from the door. "Maybe we shouldn't take this to the police. Is there anywhere we could privately test for prints?"

"Privately test for prints," Mark said in a tone that suggested I was talking crazy talk. "I don't even know if that's possible. What's going on?"

"What if the chief is the one who sent the note?"

Mark finished pulling on his coat. "He's the chief of police. He's not going to send you a note to try to stop you from investigating this case."

"Because a chief of police would never do that." I couldn't keep the sarcasm from my voice. My first experience with the Fair Haven PD had involved a chief of police who did that and more to keep me from poking my nose where he felt it didn't belong.

Mark sighed. "I would recognize Chief McTavish's handwriting. It wasn't his."

I opened a cabinet drawer, pulled out a freezer bag, dropped the envelope in, and sealed it with more force than was necessary. Mark wouldn't lie to me, and that left me with no choice but to trust that he was right. But I didn't have to like it.

Mark was already on his phone, talking to someone about us needing to speak with the chief right away, that we were coming to the station.

That fact that he hadn't waited for me to agree felt a little like a betrayal. I brushed past him and out the door. Mark followed behind me without a word.

The short, cold walk to the truck cooled my temper off a bit. I'd gotten to like my independence from someone else telling me how to live since coming to Fair Haven. It wasn't surprising that it'd be hard for me to adjust to being part of a couple where decisions would once again be made together and where I'd have someone willing to step on my toes occasionally if it was in my best interest.

And the part of my brain that wasn't panicking over another murderer taking note of me or throwing a childish hissy fit over Mark's dictatorial action knew he was right. I buckled my seatbelt and waited for Mark to pull out onto the road. "Even if he didn't write it—"

Mark sent me a withering sidelong glance that said, *Really?*

I crossed my arms and slumped back into the seat. "Even though he didn't write it, Chief McTavish is going to use this as another reason for me to stay away from the case. I have every right as Holly's lawyer to be looking into things."

"Maybe he's right," Mark said so softly it was almost lost under the whine of the tires on the pavement. "Maybe you should stop investigating."

The fury in my gut that had died down to embers flamed up again and sent enough heat through me that I felt like I could shoot dragon fire from my nostrils. "If I didn't know your handwriting, I might think you sent the note."

Mark huffed another sigh, longer and carrying more frustration this time. "All I'm saying is that you're very good at what you do, and that keeps putting you in danger." The annoyance drained out of his voice. "I don't want to lose you."

Underneath the annoyance in his voice was another note, one I hadn't heard before. Fear.

When we were together, it was sometimes easy to forget he'd been widowed once already. The situations were entirely different, but the pain of it wouldn't be. My propensity for falling headlong into dangerous situations despite my best efforts to the contrary could very well give him second thoughts about pursuing anything permanent with me. No sane man would want to experience that level of emotional pain again.

But I couldn't agree to drop this case. Worse, I wasn't sure how to explain to him why. It went beyond my sense of duty to fulfill the promise I made to Nancy. There was this piece inside me that wanted to keep going. And that scared me worse than the note did.

I stretched my hand across the seat toward him, and he took it, calling a temporary truce.

We rode in silence the rest of the way to the police station.

One of the Fair Haven officers I didn't know well waited for us in the lobby. He and Mark exchanged pleasantries as he led us to the chief's office.

The call to enter came almost in unison with the officer's knock.

The office seemed to change very little with each new resident. I'd visited it more times in the past half year than anyone who wasn't a police officer should have. The main change since Chief McTavish took over seemed to be the cluster of small pictures on his desk. I couldn't see what they were of, but the smart money would be on his family. The rest of the room was stark and clinical, almost like he didn't want to settle in.

"Show me this note," he said in place of a hello.

I handed him the freezer bag. He snapped on a pair of latex gloves and eased the letter out. He barely seemed to glance at it before sliding it back in, replacing it into the bag, and removing the gloves.

He leaned on the arm of his chair and looked at us without speaking. The tick of the wall clock grew so loud that I wanted to stick my fingers in my ears to block it out.

But I wouldn't give him the satisfaction because I knew the game he was playing. The question was whether he knew that I saw right through him or if he still thought I was some silly glory-hunter.

Two could play at his game. I crossed my legs in a way that said I don't have anywhere better to be and waited.

At least a minute passed with Mark shifting uncomfortably in his chair and watching our showdown. I could almost hear him wondering if he should say something.

Chief McTavish slid the freezer bag back across the desk. "It's not a threat. In fact, it's actually quite polite and sounds worried about you. It could as easily have been sent by someone completely unconnected to the case. It'd be a waste to use up department resources to process this."

All of Mark's discomfort vanished, and the capable medical examiner returned. "You don't really believe that, Chief."

He turned cold eyes in my direction. "What I believe is that she likely wrote the note herself."

Mark started to protest, and McTavish held up his hand. "I know your message said you were with her, but she could have planted it earlier."

I snaked my hand out and grabbed a pen and a piece of paper from the corner of his desk before he could react. I wrote out the same words as were on the letter and ice-skated it back across the desk to him. "Does it look like the handwriting matches?"

I knew I was losing my control, and I could hear all the reprimands my parents had ever given me playing a litany in my head, but this was ridiculous. I wasn't some sort of crazy person.

Somewhere along the way, we'd both gotten to our feet. I didn't remember standing up.

Mark rose slowly and patted the air like he wanted to wave a white flag. "I think you two don't get along because you're a little too much alike in some ways.

She suspected that you'd written the note, Chief, and I had to convince her to bring it in."

For the first time, McTavish's composure slipped. He dipped his chin. "I will acknowledge that I might have unjustly accused you of sending the note." He dropped back into his chair. "I've spent most of my career in departments where corruption was suspected or where they'd proven it and someone needed to pick up the pieces afterward. You start to see ghosts after a while."

Olive branch offered. I was willing to accept it. I sat as well. "It's the same as a criminal lawyer. You know of so many people who are guilty and pretending to be innocent that you start assuming everyone is guilty of something. But I didn't write that note."

McTavish handed the freezer bag to Mark.

My chest hollowed slightly. After all that, was he still sending us away without checking for prints?

"Ask them to log that in and have it dusted," McTavish said. "I'd like to talk to your girlfriend alone for a minute."

Mark met my gaze and quirked an eyebrow, an unspoken *you okay with that?*

I nodded. Somehow McTavish and I needed to find a way to work together civilly. I couldn't do my job for Holly if he was treating me like someone who was capable of tampering with a murder investigation.

The door clicked softly shut, signaling Mark's exit.

McTavish ran his fingers across his knuckles. "I looked into you, Ms. *Fitzhenry-Dawes.*"

The way he sneered my last name seemed to have nothing to do with why most people reacted to my hyphenated last name.

I bit down hard on the inside of my cheek to keep from sneering his last name in return. I'd already stooped to his level once too often, something Mark had risked pointing out even though I hadn't wanted to listen. "After looking me up, you still believe I'd be capable of impeding an investigation and fabricating evidence?"

"After looking you up, I believe you'd be capable of anything to win."

I'd have preferred it if he'd thrown a punch at me. At least I could have tried to block it. His words tunneled right inside and battered my heart into a pulp.

If he knew he'd hurt my feelings, he didn't let on.

"It'll be better for everyone if you realize now that I'm not the type of officer to be bullied or intimidated by a lawyer who'll do anything to free her client, even hurt good people, just like that note said." He splayed his hands flat on the desk. "Everyone has the right to a defense. It's part of what makes our legal system great. But that doesn't mean I have to respect the lawyers who defend clients they know are guilty."

Queasiness welled up in my stomach. When he said he'd looked me up, he didn't mean anything I'd done here in Fair Haven. He meant he'd looked up my credentials to practice law, which led him to my parents' firm, with its reputation for defending people who were clearly guilty.

For a second I considered defending what little honor they had—my parents never tampered with evidence or did anything outright illegal. In fact, they'd have sued anyone for slander who even suggested it.

But their integrity wasn't the real point here. Mine was. And he didn't believe I had any.

At least now I understood what I was up against. I'd always preferred that to not knowing.

I slowly rose to my feet. "If you believe that's the kind of lawyer I am, then you didn't do your homework well enough." I nudged my chin toward the copy of the note I'd written. "If you wouldn't mind, I'd like a photocopy of the note when you're finished checking it for prints. You might think it's a fake, but I prefer not to take chances when lives are at risk."

Chapter 14

The only thing that kept me from crying when Mark brought me home after my confrontation with Chief McTavish, or from crying when I was alone in my room that night, was knowing what my mother would say.

Lawyers don't cry because someone doesn't like them, Nicole.

To compensate, the next day, I ate too many of the candy samples Nancy wanted me to approve for the gift baskets and completely negated the salad I'd choked down the day before. Not that I had anything against salads normally. It's just that a salad doesn't exactly scream *comfort food* when you've had a bad day. To add insult to indigestion, I'd made too much and ended up having to eat it for lunch again.

As I was loading my dishes into the dishwasher afterward, Daisy called to tell me Holly was awake, but the doctors weren't allowing anyone to question her yet because of her medical condition. I regretted that for the Northgates' sake, but selfishly I was glad for a reprieve from facing Chief McTavish again. As much as I wanted everyone to like me, I could handle not being liked. That was inevitable in life for everyone. What I couldn't stand was unfair criticism. I'd worked so hard to prove I wasn't like my parents, and he'd whisked it all away like it didn't matter.

At least Mark had promised to follow up on getting me a copy of the letter if Chief McTavish didn't. After yesterday's confrontation, I wouldn't put it past him to withhold it simply to spite me.

Given my mood, I decided that what I really needed was to take the rest of the day off with my dogs and a copy of the must-read mystery Mandy recommended. I settled in on the couch, and Toby crawled up beside me. As hard as I'd tried to keep him off my furniture, his first owner, Bonnie, had let him sleep wherever he wanted. Today I welcomed the comfort. Velma curled up on the dog bed next to us and laid her head—cone and all—on my feet.

The characters in the book had barely discovered the body when my doorbell rang. Both dogs were on their feet and across the house before I could even close the book.

A little tingle crept up the back of my neck. I wasn't expecting anyone, and most people would assume I'd be somewhere else on Sugarwood property this time of day. I fished my cell out of the couch crack it'd slid into when Toby launched himself off and took it with me. If it was anyone associated with Drew's case outside my door, or anyone I didn't recognize, I could call Mark and keep him on speakerphone until they were gone. Better safe than dead.

I squished an eye to my door's peephole and received a magnified view of Quincey Dornbush's bald head and part of his face.

I slumped against the door. Thank goodness.

I unlocked the door—after finding that note, no one was convincing me to leave it unlocked ever—and stepped outside to protect Quincey's uniform from doggie drool.

He held up a brown nine-by-twelve envelope. "The chief asked me to bring this to you."

His look clearly said *why am I always the messenger?* But in a good-natured way. He was probably just grateful he hadn't been asked to transport my extremely feminine and flamboyant luggage again.

I accepted the envelope and looked inside. It held the photocopy of the note that I'd requested.

He took a step backward as if he was anxious to dispatch his carrier pigeon duties and get back to work.

"He also wanted you to know that they didn't find any fingerprints on it. If you receive any other messages, he'd like you to bring them in."

Interesting. Mark wasn't going to ask about the note unless I hadn't received word by the end of the week. This delivery must have come from Chief McTavish without prompting.

I'd never trusted the old saying of *don't look a gift horse in the mouth*. Not looking was exactly how the people of Troy lost their city to the Greeks.

All I said to Quincey was, "Thank you. I will."

He tipped his hat and double-timed it back to his car.

Back inside the house, I laid the photocopy out on my counter. It was a strange situation. The sender knew enough to protect against fingerprints, but they hadn't taken the extra precaution of printing the note rather than handwriting it. While fingerprints would have been easier and more conclusive, that meant I still had a lead to follow. If I could get a sample of each male tour member's handwriting, I could compare it to see if it looked similar. I wasn't a trained graphologist, but I'd always had an eye for detail.

I worried the edge of the envelope. How could I get samples of their handwriting? It'd be a bit obvious to walk up and ask for it. That wouldn't tip the note-sender off at *all*.

I did have a small sample of George Powers' and Ted Marshall's writing. They'd both signed in to the tour guest book with their name and hometown. Unfortunately, Kristen White signed the book for her family while Shawn was paying. Maybe that wouldn't matter. I might get lucky and find one of the samples I had matched the note—if you could call it lucky to find out a sick man or a newly married man had killed someone.

I put Velma back in her crate since her incision wasn't looking any better than it had last week and dressed Toby in the plaid dog coat I'd bought for him. Finding the doggie jackets had been surprisingly challenging. Every pet store sold them for small dogs, but I'd had to special order ones online that would fit my dogs. It was worth it, though, to see them cozy on our walks. If I found the Michigan weather cold in my winter gear, they must, too.

I snatched up the note and set off with Toby toward the rental shop. Tour guests all checked in there to pay and sign the book before heading out.

When we reached the shop, I hooked Toby's leash to the old-fashioned hitching post out front since I'd learned the hard way that not everyone liked big dogs. The last time I'd brought him into the rental shop, the guests inside shrank back and refused to pass by like they thought he was going to tear away from me and eat them.

It turned out I could have brought Toby inside. The shop was empty except for Dave, his gangly form hunched over a pad of paper, gnawing on the end of a pencil.

He grinned at me around the pencil. "Do you need me for something? I'm in the middle of an exciting scene."

I waved him back to his work. In the past two months, Dave had given me three different novel beginnings to read. Unfortunately, he kept getting stuck three or four chapters in, and I was left wondering what would happen to all the people he'd introduced me to. It was surprisingly frustrating. If he was making it further on this story, I didn't want to interrupt him.

I tiptoed around him, snagged the guest book, and brought it to the far end of the counter. Since no tours had run since the one on which Drew died, the entries were the last in the book.

I laid my paper out beside the correct page. The first entry read *George and Amy Powers, Fair Haven, Michigan.*

George Powers' handwriting filled the line and spilled over into the next one in big, sloppy loops that almost looked like he struggled to control the pen. Knowing what I did now, he probably had been struggling to control the pen.

That wasn't the only difference, though. George Powers' entry connected letters like O, V, and W down low, in a very distinct pattern, whereas the writer of the letter connected them high, more like my own handwriting.

The handwriting on the note I'd been sent was also neater and smaller, with a more noticeable slant to the left.

Mr. Marshall had signed the line below, which was actually two lines below, since George Powers hadn't been able to stay on one line.

Ted and Janet Marshall, it read. *Cincinnati, Ohio.*

Not only was his handwriting much too dark for the note I'd received—he'd almost punched through the thick guest book paper with how much pressure he applied—but his letters were all points and sharp edges. The writing in the note had a smoother flow.

Kristen White's entry, as expected, didn't match, either, though hers came the closest.

I whopped the guest book closed and flinched. I'd probably frightened Dave right out of his train of thought. When I looked up, he didn't seem to have noticed, and the eraser on his pencil now lay in pink confetti bits all around his paper.

I bid him goodbye, but his wave was so distracted that I had a suspicion he'd look up an hour from now and wonder where I'd gone.

The note safely back in my pocket, I retrieved Toby. I'd have sworn he looked at me reproachfully for leaving him out in the fresh snow for two minutes while I'd been inside. I brought us home by the long way since the sun actually felt almost warm, and it gave me time to think about my next step.

If the person who killed Drew had sent me the note, then I had to work under the assumption that the note writer-killer was also a man on the tour. Since Ted Marshall's and George Powers' handwriting didn't match, that narrowed it down to Kristen's husband Shawn. The conundrum there was he didn't have a motive that I'd seen yet, and he'd had his little boy with him as far as I knew. This was beginning to feel like a Sherlock Holmes' locked room mystery, and instead of Sherlock in this scenario, I was Dr. Watson, stumbling around, unable to see the clues that must be right in front of me.

I supposed that theoretically none of them had done it. Amy did text a drug dealer who might have had a good reason to want Drew dead with the information that she'd be on a tour at Sugarwood. But that brought me back to the original dilemma that we'd have been almost impossible to find out in the bush unless someone knew where to look and had a way to sneak in and out while we were all actively paying attention to our surroundings because we were looking for Riley. Given the spotty cell reception in the area and that Amy hadn't said she'd communicated with the dealer directly before, that seemed highly unlikely.

So even though I couldn't yet explain away how Shawn had killed Drew while carrying his son or figure out what his motive was, I still needed to see if his handwriting matched the note.

Kristen had told me Shawn was a high school teacher, so if I hurried, I might be able to make it to the school right as class was letting out and before he'd erased the chalkboard. That'd be a safe place to do it as well. If he was the killer, he wouldn't risk hurting me in a school teeming with students and other teachers.

If the note writer-killer wasn't someone on the tour, I'd have a whole new problem on my hands, because even I couldn't come up with a good enough story to convince Mark that poking into the business of a drug dealer would be perfectly safe and reasonable.

The posted policy on the school door I entered said all visitors had to check in at the front desk. Surely that only meant during school hours. That'd be my excuse if someone questioned me on it, anyway, because I didn't have time to check in, nor did I want Shawn coming to the office to meet me.

I had to stop three kids before one of them could direct me to his room. Not exactly keeping a low profile, though I'd bet none of them wanted to take the time to report an interloper to the office even if they did suspect I hadn't checked in.

Room 103 turned out to be a science room, if the sinks in the desks and the row of practically antique Bunsen burners along the shelves were any indication. Shawn had his back to the door, facing a projector. A projector screen covered the chalkboard.

I groaned inside. I'd planned to stop by under the guise of offering his family a free tour, and now I might have to stall. And pray that he'd used the chalkboard sometime today.

I rapped my knuckled against the door frame.

He turned around, and an expression I couldn't quite interpret flickered across his face. It was probably nothing more than that he'd been expecting a student, and I clearly wasn't that. It disappeared as quickly as it'd been there.

Seeing him now, apart from his winter gear, he was the kind of teacher that all the female students probably had a crush on, tall and lean, with blue eyes and a haircut that did a good job of hiding his slightly receding hairline.

"Kristen did give me your message, and I meant to give you a call last week, but I've been grading exams." He pointed to a pile of papers on the corner of his desk. His cell phone and keys rested on top like paperweights. "Still ongoing, as you can see, and I don't think I have anything useful to add to your hunt."

That's right. I had asked Kristen to have him call me. I'd forgotten to follow up when he didn't call back. If I pursued that now, though, he'd find it suspicious when I tried to get a look at his chalkboard.

"Actually, I came because I wanted to offer your family a free tour to make up for the...eventful one you had last time." Why wouldn't I have simply told Kristen that? Why would I have had to make a trip here to offer it when I knew their phone number? "I, uh, didn't want to offer it to Kristen in case the kids overheard. I thought it might be something the two of you would want to decide."

That sounded plausible, right? I smiled to add believability to my words.

He gave an upward-chin-jut nod. "Thanks. I'll talk it over with her."

He took the Bunsen burner off his front counter, stepped around the projector, and carried it to the far wall.

Aaand that should have ended the conversation if offering a free tour was why I'd really come, but he hadn't yet moved the projector screen. I hadn't planned for this contingency. What kind of a school used dinosaur-age projectors anyway?

"Do you need help cleaning the chalkboard?" I blurted. I stepped past the projector toward the board. "I always liked wiping them down when I was in school."

Heat snaked up my neck and into my cheeks. My mother's shame-sensors were probably going off all the way in DC. That sounded so silly even to me that my ego had cringed up into a ball inside and was dying a slow, agonizing death.

I blasted him with an even bigger smile. Maybe he'd think I was smitten with him the way his students probably were. I prayed Mark would never hear of it because he *really* didn't like when I acted interested in suspects to wheedle information out of them.

In Shawn's defense, he didn't give away that he noticed my goofiness, probably a skill you had to develop to survive as a teacher or you'd have kids complaining to their parents that their teacher had mocked them. He walked over to the screen and pulled it up. It retraced with a whoosh.

"Nope," he said. "Looks all clean."

An electric jolt zinged through me like I'd shocked myself. It wasn't all clean. He'd written a homework assignment in the corner. A dull ache replaced the jolt. If the writing on the board was his, it didn't match the handwriting on the note. I had to be sure.

My parents would never forgive me if they found out, but playing dumb seemed like the smartest move.

"I was terrible at chemistry in high school, but my parents insisted on straight A's. When I found out I'd gotten a B+, I went to my teacher and argued my way up to an A." I pointed to the writing. "Is that all for one day of your class? I don't think I would have even gotten a B as your student if it is."

My giggle could have been interpreted as either inane or unbalanced. It was a toss-up.

He gave me a tolerant smile, so it seemed like he'd heard inane. "Yup, that's what I expect them to have done for tomorrow. This is AP chemistry."

That clinched it. He couldn't have written the note either. Time to make my exit before I made an even bigger fool of myself.

I backed up a step and turned around. My ankle caught on something that felt like a thin rope and I pitched sideways toward the counter. My arms shot out to stop the fall, but I missed. My hands connected with the papers and something else more solid on the desk, sending them flying, and I smashed ribs-first into the edge of the counter.

Pain burned through my side, and all my air rushed out with an *oomph*. I barely managed to grab the counter edge in time to keep from landing in a heap. The projector wobbled precariously next to me. I must have tripped on the cord.

Shawn swore low in his throat and scrambled to my side. He stretched out his hands but didn't make contact, like he wanted to help but couldn't overcome his training on not touching students to do it. "Are you okay?"

Debatable. My ribs felt like someone had painted them with burning coals. The heat flaming in my face almost rivaled the heat in my side. Forget clumsiest person on the planet. If aliens existed, I'd win clumsiest being in the galaxy.

It was one thing to have Mark realize that—he was my boyfriend. It was quite another thing to have someone else know it and have it spread around the entire town. "I'm fine."

Breathing deeply hurt. I inched around the counter. What were the chances this was a bad bruise and not fractured ribs? I couldn't hide fractured ribs. My baby steps brought me to the end of the counter. His phone lay on the floor alongside the papers. Crap. I'd probably broken it, and I'd have to buy him a new one.

I eased as slowly as possible onto one knee, trying to keep my torso mostly straight. "Let me help you clean this up."

"Don't worry about that," Shawn was saying. "I can do it."

His phone dinged, and I swept it up. If it was still receiving texts, it couldn't be entirely destroyed. I went to pass it to him, but my gaze snagged on the screen.

A string of seemingly random letters and numbers, exactly how Amy had described the text she'd been told to send to the dealer to prove she wasn't a police officer.

I sucked in a breath and nearly dropped the phone. My hand shook slightly.

My mind screamed that I had to pull it together. Shawn couldn't have missed my reaction, and if he figured out that I knew he was dealing drugs, he could destroy any evidence of what he was doing before I could convince the police to look into him. My only hope was to pretend whatever expression he thought he saw on my face came from pain.

I handed over the phone and clutched my throbbing ribs with my other hand. "I don't feel well. The pain's getting worse. I think I should go for an x-ray."

His face didn't give away whether he believed me or not. It's a good thing all teachers weren't criminals. They had too much practice at hiding when something bothered them.

I eased up to my feet, making sure to favor my ribs even more than I was already inclined to. The best thing to do to substantiate my claim was to call someone to take me to the hospital.

The pain was making it increasingly hard to breathe, so that might be the smartest move anyway. Please God let me not have hit the counter hard enough to puncture a lung or some other vital organ. Would I still be able to stand if I'd done that much damage?

Shawn pulled his chair over to where I was. Either my ruse worked or I was starting to look pale.

"Should I call an ambulance?" he asked.

I didn't want strangers. I wanted Mark. For more reasons than one.

The part of my brain that still seemed to be thinking rationally and wasn't convinced I was about to die whispered that I should keep working to disarm Shawn's suspicion. I handed him my phone. "My boyfriend. He's a doctor. Please call him. Under Mark."

Chapter 15

"What were you doing at the school in the first place?" Mark asked as he helped me back out to my car after I'd been x-rayed and examined until I was sorry I'd come.

The doctor and Mark both agreed my ribs were only mildly fractured, not broken. I didn't seem to have any more serious damage, but I'd still need to rest.

Unfortunately, with so many people around at the hospital, I hadn't had a chance to explain how I'd ended up in a high school chemistry room and what I'd discovered.

"It's possible that I was there trying to see if Shawn's handwriting matched the writing on the note since they didn't find any fingerprints."

Mark turned one of his eyebrows into a triangle. "It's possible?"

"Depends on how mad you'll be if I admit to it."

His hands clenched around the steering wheel, turning his knuckles white. "Will you at least tell me next time before you head off into a potentially dangerous situation?"

"Will you try to stop me?"

His dimple peeked out and his grip on the steering wheel relaxed slightly. "It's possible."

"It wasn't supposed to be a dangerous situation. I did this to myself." I adjusted the seatbelt so that it didn't put as much pressure on my chest and filled Mark in on what I'd figured out. "Except it feels like I'm trying to fit together pieces that belong to two different puzzles. The text message I saw makes it look like he's the one Drew was investigating for dealing drugs, but his handwriting doesn't match the note."

"We don't know Drew was investigating anything. We're guessing. If Drew was putting together proof that Shawn was dealing, the police should have found some evidence. They took his computer, his camera, everything that could have been evidence for a motive." Mark's lips thinned. "Erik's been keeping me updated on the case, and they didn't find anything unusual."

Working through a puzzle like this with Mark again felt good. I don't think I'd realized how much I missed it in the stretch that we hadn't been speaking to each other prior to dating.

More than that, I don't think I'd realized how much I'd missed investigating in general even though the last case I'd been part of hadn't been that long ago.

A pain beat in my chest that had nothing to do with my ribs. I felt the most like myself when I was working on solving a crime. I'd come to Fair Haven, to Sugarwood, to escape being a lawyer. If Chief McTavish looked more carefully at my history, he'd see that I'd been a terrible criminal defense attorney and he'd probably want me defending all the criminals he'd like to lock away. I'd never been the lead on a case because I sounded like an awkward seventh grader with a stutter whenever I tried to speak in front of a jury. And your clientele was going to be small when you insisted on defending only the innocent. My dad had once told me they were all guilty. He'd only been a little bit wrong. Where did that leave me?

Mark was giving me a look that said he was worried about me fainting.

I pulled myself back to the problem at hand. Figuring out my life could wait. Right now, proving Holly was innocent so that she'd still have a life outside of prison was what mattered most.

"They didn't find anything in Drew's belongings." I repeated what we knew, giving my subconscious a chance to hear it again. It felt like I was stretching as far as I could reach and my mental fingers kept brushing the edge of the answer as it floated away. "They didn't find anything on Holly's computer either?"

Mark shook his head.

Maybe the police weren't the only ones looking. "Both houses were broken in to. I know the chief thinks it's part of the B&E streak that's been happening, but if it wasn't, it suggests the thief was looking for something. They managed to take the family desktop from Holly's house. Do you know what was taken from Drew's?"

"They didn't have a lot to steal, according to Erik. The Harris' were still sorting through to see if anything small had been taken the last I heard, but their computer was gone as well."

The way the corners of Mark's lips drooped down told me he saw the connection too.

I shifted around again. My chances of getting comfortable anywhere until my ribs healed seemed about as good as someone stepping forward unbidden and confessing to Drew's murder. "So assuming the thief was also connected to Drew's murder, they might have been hoping to find the evidence Drew'd collected."

"Theoretically," Mark said. "But if that's true, then whatever evidence Drew collected is gone, and we might never be able to prove who he was investigating or why."

And Holly might go to prison for a crime she didn't commit.

It turned out that large dogs with a lot of pent-up energy and a person with cracked ribs were a bad combination. My stubborn attempt to take Velma out for a bathroom break on her leash resulted in a howl of pain from me and Mark insisting he'd sleep over on the couch for a few nights to watch over me. The rumor factory would have a bestseller if anyone found out—there'd certainly be assumptions that the couch wasn't where he was sleeping—but I hurt too much to care.

Before heading out the next morning, Mark even called Russ to make sure someone would come to walk the dogs and check on me while he was at work. The text I got from Mark said not to lock my door because he didn't want me having to get up to let anyone in.

The knowledge that my door was unlocked would have been enough to keep me from resting, but by one o'clock the next afternoon, it was clear Russ had panicked about me being alone and arranged some sort of rotating schedule for the Sugarwood employees. My front door barely closed behind one visitor before another dropped in. Stacey brought a get-well card for the boy who'd been in the hit-and-run accident the week before that she was having everyone at Sugarwood sign—his dad worked for her dad. Dave read me the start to his new fantasy story, and our cook at the

Short Stack dropped off lunch. Nancy delivered snacks and the news that Holly was cleared to receive visitors, but that the chief had agreed to wait one day to question her so I could recuperate.

That was quite the concession, and the second in a row. It had to be a psychological game. He wanted me to drop my guard.

I must have dozed off after Nancy left because I woke up to knocking on my door and a mouth dry enough from the sweets she left that the dogs' water bowl almost looked appealing.

We'd had so many visitors throughout the day that Toby didn't even break his snore. Velma lifted her coned head for a half-hearted woof and continued slurpily licking her stuffed monkey.

"Come in," I called and shimmied back up into a sitting position. I probably had an atrocious case of couch-cushion head, but I'd discovered this morning that raising my arms up felt about as comfortable as popping one of my ribs right out. It was probably Russ anyway since the clock said it was close to the time the dogs would need another trip outside.

Instead of Russ, Kristen came in, followed closely by Shawn.

I instinctively raised a hand to my hair and bit back a yelp. I sucked in a rapid breath and nearly keeled over. I had to be more careful. My mind slowly cleared to the realization that a possible murderer-drug dealer was in my home.

I started to reach for my phone just in case—I couldn't have even fought off a two-year-old in my current state—but rational thought returned before I found it. My dogs were here, and Kristen probably had no idea what her husband was doing on the side. Even if he did suspect I'd figured out the truth, he wasn't going to do anything with her around. I'd just have to make the long trip across the room to lock the door after them once they left.

Kristen's walk would have been better described as a slink, as if she were afraid of my reaction to them. "I hope we didn't wake you."

No, my hair always looks like this is what I wanted to say, but I was certain she'd interpret that as snottiness rather than as teasing. "That's no problem. I'm supposed to take deep breaths every so often anyway, and it's hard to make sure I'm doing that if I'm asleep."

Kristen flinched. "Shawn told me about what happened, and we wanted to bring a little care package." She pulled a card and a bottle of ibuprofen out of her bag and passed them to me. She pointed to the card. "There's a gift card in there to download some audiobooks. In case you get bored. I thought listening would be easier on you than trying to hold up a book."

She mimicked holding a book with her upper arms plastered to her sides. It took every ounce of self-control not to crack up, and, horrible as it sounds, I did it more for the sake of my ribs than for her. People got so goofy around someone who was "sick."

She glanced back at Shawn and her eyes did that rapid sideways movement that said *your turn*.

He looked less contrite than Kristen, but he stepped forward on cue anyway. "I wanted to apologize on behalf of myself and the school. I should have been more careful about the cord."

I drew in the slow, deep breath the doctor had instructed me to. He said it would seem counterintuitive, and it did, but, apparently, it decreased my risk of pneumonia or a lung collapse, both complications I'd love to avoid. It did increase the throbbing ache, though. I rubbed a hand over my side, and Kristen shot a frightened rabbit look at Shawn.

And then I got it. They were afraid I was going to sue Shawn, the high school, or both. "It was really nice of you to come, but there's no need to feel bad. I should have been paying more attention."

Based on the way Kristen's shoulders came down from their position near her ears, that eased her fears at least a little.

"Can we get you something else before we leave?" Shawn asked. "Something to eat?"

After the giant lunch of sausage and pancakes I'd had from the Short Stack and the array of sweets Nancy dropped off, food was the last thing I needed, but a drink sounded great. "A glass of something to drink would be nice. Anything from the fridge."

Shawn headed for the kitchen.

Kristen came to stand beside me. Up close, I could see she wasn't wearing any makeup. This whole situation must have upset her even more than I realized. She'd done her makeup even for the tour out into the sugar bush.

"I really am sorry. Shawn was sloppy."

You'd think I was in critical condition with how solemn she looked. "Don't worry about it. You couldn't have known this was going to happen any more than I could have anticipated what happened on the tour."

For a second I thought she might argue with me again, but Shawn returned and set a glass of grape juice on the table beside me. "If there's anything else we can do for you, let us know."

He took Kristen by the arm and led her toward the door. She glanced back over her shoulder at me one more time and gave a feeble wave.

As soon as the door closed behind them, I picked myself up off the couch and shuffled to the door. I flipped the lock. Russ had a spare key, and I'd given Mark my set. I didn't need any other visitors at this point.

I'd barely made it back to the couch before a key turned in the lock and Russ came in for the dogs. I really should have known better. A revolving door would make more sense than a lock at this point. Still, I had him lock the door on his way out.

All the movement and the talking had made my ribs feel like the blood in my body was pooling there and pulsing. The area practically vibrated with pain. I poured two ibuprofen out of the bottle Kristen and Shawn brought me—the doctor had prescribed me some but I'd accidentally left it upstairs this morning—and gulped them down with half the grape juice.

The juice tasted off, almost bitter. I hadn't bought the bottle that long ago, so I must have left it sitting out too long at some point. I returned the glass, still half full, to the side table, and nestled back into my cushions. I leaned my head on my pillow.

A text dinged on my phone. I couldn't be sure whether I'd drifted off or not.

Have to work late, Mark wrote, *but my mom is on her way to make you supper.*

Normally I would have felt awkward letting my boyfriend's mom who I'd never met take care of me, but considering how many people had been in and out of my home already today, it almost seemed normal. Hopefully Mark had given her the keys. He might not have since he'd expected me to leave the door unlocked.

I tried to write a reply about the keys, but my blood pounded behind my eyes and the phone slipped from my hand as if I'd been trying to hold a twenty-five pound weight rather than a phone that weighed only a few grams. Cramps flared across my abdomen.

Something was wrong.

Chapter 16

Panic crawled up my throat and made it difficult to breathe. This didn't feel like food poisoning from spoiled grape juice. It didn't feel like the symptoms the doctor had warned me could signal a complication with my ribs, either.

Thunder rattled my door. Was there a storm?

No, not a storm. Someone was knocking. Pounding. On my door.

"Nicole, it's Mrs. Cavanaugh," a woman's voice called. "Mark sent me. Can you unlock the door for me?"

She didn't have my keys. She couldn't get to me. My throat felt raw, almost like I'd swallowed powdered glass, and my voice came out in a croak. Velma whined, a pitiful keening sound, and Toby nudged at me with a cold nose.

"Nicole!" A note of concern had entered Mrs. Cavanaugh's voice. "Are you alright?"

I scooted along the couch. It might as well have been a marathon with how weak my body felt. All I could think was that I was going to die here alone if I couldn't get to the door and the first glimpse of me Mark's mom would get was when they wheeled my corpse out on a stretcher.

I reached the end of the couch and pushed to my feet, the shriek of my fractured ribs dull compared to the raging in the rest of my body. I took one step and my legs gave out. I fell back into the couch. The door was too far away.

Mrs. Cavanaugh might go away if she thought I was asleep. I had to find some way to signal her. Tell her that I was in trouble. My vocal cords seemed to lack the strength to call out.

With as much force as I could muster, I knocked over the new lamp I'd bought to replace the one Velma broke. It crashed to the floor.

"I'm calling for help," the voice on the other side of the door shouted, "and I'm going to get in to you somehow."

She sounded farther away this time. I couldn't tell if she actually was or if my hearing was fading. The room around me spun like someone had dropped me into a blender.

The door flew open, and Mrs. Cavanaugh sprinted across the house, her skirt flapping around her legs, my clearly-obvious hide-a-key rock in her hand. She dropped the rock halfway to me.

I tried to stand, fell into her arms, and threw up all over her shirt.

My next clear memory, I was riding in an ambulance, sirens blaring above me, an IV in my arm, and Mrs. Cavanaugh was trying to answer questions she couldn't possibly know the answer to.

I closed my eyes, and when I opened them again, I wasn't moving anymore and the walls were farther away than an ambulance's would be. I didn't remember passing out, but I must have. My body felt more normal again, still a little weak but the pain had located back in my ribs where it belonged.

I shifted my head on the pillow. Mark sat in a chair beside my bed, head bowed over folded hands like he was praying.

"Please tell me I only dreamed I barfed on your mom," I said.

Mark's head snapped up. He grabbed both sides of my face and kissed me hard on the forehead, then on the lips. "Thank God you're awake."

I guess even doctors weren't calmer or more confident than anyone else when it was someone they cared about in the hospital. His reaction also meant it was a safe bet I hadn't imagined the whole throw-up-on-my-boyfriend's-mom thing. That was so much worse than meeting her covered in dog slobber. What I wouldn't give for a *Harry Potter* Time-Turner right about now. Though if I had one, I'd change a lot more than simply vomiting on Mark's mom. "What's wrong with me? Was it my ribs?"

Mark sank back into his chair. If it wasn't a complete impossibility, I'd think he had a few more gray hairs now than he had when I saw him this morning—assuming it was still the same day. I could have been out for a week for all I knew.

He linked his fingers through mine and adjusted the bed so I could comfortably sit up. "You had dangerously high levels of nicotine in your system. My mom got to you in time, but you could have died."

He didn't have to say that someone had tried to kill me. Again. It was a given since I didn't smoke or have any other sources of nicotine in my house. Maybe I should have felt scared, or remorseful for not listening to Mark's concerns that this could happen, or shocked. But I didn't. All I felt was angry. How could so many people think this was an okay way to solve their problems?

But ranting wasn't going to get us anywhere, and my parents had raised me to be practical if nothing else. "Did they find out how I ingested the poison?" Since my body tried to get rid of it, it seemed like a safe bet I'd eaten it rather than taking it in through my skin.

"It was in your grape juice. Chief McTavish wants a list of everyone who's been in your house lately."

I snorted, which got me a confused smile from Mark. "About half the town was in my house today." But most of them hadn't been anywhere near my kitchen. Only three, in fact. One was Mark, who I knew hadn't tried to kill me. "Our cook from the Short Stack brought me lunch, and she could have done it, but she wouldn't have a reason to. But I also had a visit from Shawn and Kristen White. He got me the glass of juice. Didn't the chief find his fingerprints?"

"He did, but the nicotine was in the bottle of juice, too, not just the glass. Shawn claims he didn't know anything about it, and since it was in the bottle, we can't prove otherwise." He gave my hand an extra squeeze. "Before you ask, yes, I did tell Chief McTavish about your suspicions about Drew and Shawn. Without any solid evidence, we're deadlocked."

Poisoning the bottle rather than the glass—smart. He'd covered his tracks in case I somehow lived. "Just once, it'd be nice to deal with a stupid criminal."

A muscle pulsed in Mark's jaw like he was clenching his teeth. "I'd rather you didn't deal with any more criminals at all."

I dropped my gaze to our interlinked hands. Coming back to this topic eventually had been inevitable. The reprieve the other day couldn't last, especially given how I'd ended up here. "I don't know what to tell you."

"Why you keep doing it would be a good place to start."

It was a fair question, but I'd only begun working through it myself. A normal person would have quit after the first time someone tried to kill her. "What I didn't like about being a lawyer was trying to pretend people were innocent when they were guilty. With the cases I've been a part of here, I've been doing something worthwhile. And I'm good at it."

What I wasn't good at was all the other parts of being a lawyer. Even prosecuting attorneys spent a large amount of their time in court trying cases. I wouldn't ever be good at that, and it'd be irresponsible of me to try cases that would be lost due to my ineptitude rather than due to the guilt or innocence of the defendant.

Tears built up in my head. I sniffed them down. Crying doesn't achieve anything, my dad would say. Even as a little girl, I hadn't been allowed to cry. When most people cried, we found solutions. Except I couldn't see one here. "I've been happier than I've ever been since coming to Fair Haven, but I don't know if I'll be content to spend my whole life making maple syrup."

He smoothed my mangled hair. "I love you. I don't want to lose you."

My heart did a weird little jitterbug in my chest. It was the first time Mark had said he loved me. But it felt like it was coming with a *but*. I braced myself for an ultimatum—either you stop investigating crimes or we break up. It didn't come. As much as it scared him to see me in danger, he wasn't going to take from me something that I'd started to think was at the core of who I was.

What I'd felt for Mark for so long finally came out in words. "I love you, too."

He leaned in for another kiss, but this time I was awake enough to remember I hadn't had a toothbrush in who knows how long and the last thing I'd done was expel all the food in my stomach. I slid a hand between our lips, and his mouth hit my knuckles.

"I don't suppose anyone brought my toothbrush," I said from behind my fingers.

He laughed, moved my hand, and kissed me anyway. "I don't have an answer for your career, but we'll work on a solution together. For now, can you be more careful about how you go about things? We spend too much time together in the hospital."

That was an understatement. "I'll try my best."

Mark flashed me the dimple that still set fireflies loose in my stomach. "And don't let Shawn White into your house again, no matter who he has with him or how innocent he seems."

Good Lord. How could I have missed it? Shawn White. SW. The SD card that Drew's mom brought me might not have pictures of Sugarwood on it at all.

Chapter 17

I hadn't bothered looking at the SD card Drew's mom gave me. The original disc from Drew had so many images on it that I'd found all I needed to launch the new website even without hiring another photographer right away.

I had to get back to my house and check the SD card, but I was trapped here by the IV still in my arm. I stuck my arm out toward Mark. "I need this out. I need to go home. I think I might know how to tie Shawn White to Drew's murder."

"I'm not taking that out." Mark pushed my arm gently back to my side. "And you're not going anywhere until the doctor says you can. Tell me what you're talking about and I'll go look for it."

"The police didn't get all of Drew's records, and neither did whoever broke into his house and Holly's. Drew's mom brought me a camera memory card that she thought was full of Sugarwood pictures. But she hadn't looked at it, and neither did I. The SW on the card could as easily stand for Shawn White as it could for Sugarwood."

Mark rubbed the finger where his wedding ring used to be. It was still strange to me to see it naked. "It wouldn't be enough to arrest him, but it should be enough for a warrant."

I bobbed my head. I told him where to find the card and my laptop. He was back in thirty minutes. If I was right, Chief McTavish wouldn't need to wait for me to recover to question Holly. Holly wouldn't be a suspect anymore.

Mark rested the laptop on my lap and pulled his chair as close as possible. We slid the card in.

My computer queued the pictures up.

Drew hadn't owned a telephoto lens, so the first pictures were far off and grainy, showing only a man who had a similar height and build to Shawn White with other people.

Drew must have realized those grainy long shots wouldn't get him anywhere and had picked a better place for a stakeout. The next pictures looked like they'd been taken through a car window, but they were close enough to clearly identify Shawn White. In some of them, the faces of the kids he was taking money from and handing small bags to were even visible.

There were nearly two hundred images on the card. It seemed like Drew had been following Shawn White for a while, collecting evidence until he felt like he'd have enough to prove his accusations.

It was more than enough to get a warrant. If the police could ID the other people in the pictures and convince one of them to talk, not only would they have a conviction for drug dealing, but they'd also have strong motive for him killing Drew.

I looked up at Mark. "I think it's time to call Chief McTavish."

The next day, I'd just finished changing into a fresh set of clothes Mark had brought me on his way to work when a soft knock came from the doorway of my room.

Chief McTavish stood one step inside my room, holding his hat in his hands. "I have some news about the case, and considering your assistance, I thought it was only right to share it with you."

The words came out jerky, like they were choking him. I wasn't a gloater, but it was a bit hard considering our history.

I motioned to the chair next to my bed and eased my way back up onto the bed myself.

He sat and rested his hat on his knees. "I assume you're recovered," he said, as if he'd just now realized it might be polite to ask how I was.

I was fine with skipping the small talk. "Did you get a warrant?"

"For his house, his classroom, and his phone. We didn't find anything, but we didn't really expect to. If he was concerned enough to poison you, he'd have known there was a chance we'd eventually be able to get a warrant. He even bought himself a new phone, claiming he lost his old one."

The names I wanted to call Shawn were anything but ladylike, but Chief McTavish didn't look frustrated. In fact, if he'd smiled, I might have seen canary feathers hanging from his teeth. "I think you might be enjoying keeping me in suspense, Chief."

That earned me a small smile. "The principal identified two of the teenagers in the photos, and both of them turned on White in exchange for community service."

The grin that split my face was so big it hurt my cheeks. "Did he confess after you told him that?"

"In a manner of speaking." The corners of Chief McTavish's mouth turned down. "He took a plea but he defended what he'd done, like he was doing a public service because he knew the kids were going to try it. He could give them safe product and make sure they were using it responsibly, he said. He kept track of how much and when they purchased to help prevent over-dosing. Claimed it was no different than sex ed."

The thought of him thinking he'd been doing a good thing brought a bad taste to the back of my mouth. "What about poisoning me?"

"Unfortunately, he's stonewalling us on that, and we didn't find anything to tie him to it. Yet, anyway. I have officers out to all the locations that sell any nicotine products in the area. Hopefully someone will remember selling him something. He doesn't smoke, so it'd be hard to explain why he bought something he didn't plan to use."

He'd left out the most important charge. "And Drew's murder? I'm guessing he wouldn't confess to that, either."

"Nope. And that one's going to be hard to make stick even with the proof that Drew was spying on him and meant to turn him in. He says he had no idea Drew was photographing him, so he wouldn't have had a motive. Plus, his wife insists they weren't apart long enough that day, and that he had their son with him the whole time."

A needle prick hit my heart. How much had Kristen known about all this? And when did she know? She'd seemed so nice and open the day of the tour that it made my brain ache to think that she'd known the whole time. Then again, she'd also been more upset than the situation merited when they visited my home. It was possible she'd known what Shawn planned to do, but hadn't felt like she'd had any way to stop him. She clearly loved him and loved their kids. She might have chosen to sacrifice me over losing her provider husband and her children's father to prison for ratting on him.

I smoothed the bedsheets on either side of my legs. Or Kristen was telling the truth about Shawn's inability to kill Drew. The thought made my skin want to crawl off my body in frustration because it was plausible. Kristen hadn't had their son when she returned to the clearing with Riley. Shawn would have needed super speed to return to the clearing, kill Drew, hide his gloves, and make it back deep enough into the woods to retrieve their son from Kristen.

That left Holly, the Powerses, and the Marshalls. Holly was too short, though that was all she had speaking in favor of her innocence.

Amy Powers was too small, George Powers was too frail, his handwriting hadn't matched the note, and neither of them had a motive. He wasn't hiding a drug addiction the way I'd thought, and Drew obviously hadn't planned to reveal what Amy wanted to do. He didn't have to warn her the way he did.

Mr. and Mrs. Marshall were both too short, and they'd been together the whole time. Even if they hadn't been, Mr. Marshall's handwriting hadn't matched, either, and even my suspicious mind couldn't come up with a reason they'd have wanted to kill someone they'd only recently met.

I clasped a hand around the cold metal of the bed railing. Maybe Chief McTavish had come up with a solution and he was waiting for me to ask. "So you're basically telling me that no one on the tour could have killed Drew."

"Not quite. If you're feeling well enough, I need you to come with me to speak with Holly. Otherwise, we need to assign a public defender. Either way, you should be aware that I plan to take her into custody on the charge of killing Drew Harris."

Chapter 18

Chief McTavish went to find my doctor so I could be discharged early.

Apparently, Holly's doctor had decided she was well enough to leave, and while McTavish came to talk to me, he also sent an officer to Holly's room to bring her down to the station. It felt like a sneak attack meant to prevent anyone from warning Holly what was coming. They were taking precautions to make sure she didn't run again.

Despite telling me he'd have to arrest Holly, he hadn't done it yet, but he'd flagged his intention. Unless something drastic changed in the next couple of hours during her interrogation, she'd be arrested and, soon after, brought before a judge for her plea. I had no choice but to check out of the hospital now.

Mark wasn't going to like it. He didn't want me leaving the hospital until the doctor thought I could safely go, and this morning, the doctor had told me he wanted me to stay one more night for observation.

The part of me that didn't want to be controlled by anyone sat like a devil on my shoulder, telling me to text Mark from the police cruiser when it was too late to undo what I'd done.

A much softer voice said that would create a wound in our relationship that we might not be able to heal. It'd show him that my promises meant nothing.

I dialed his number. He answered, and I explained the situation. "I'll stay if you want me to, but I'd like to remain on this case."

The long-suffering sigh I'd been dreading didn't come.

"Most public defenders already have an impossible case load," he said instead. "If she's passed off to them, they'll encourage her to take a plea because the evidence makes it look like mounting a defense would be a waste of time."

Chief McTavish was coming down the hall, my doctor at his side. I angled away slightly. "That's what I'm afraid of. What should I do?"

"Go."

"You're sure?"

"Yeah. But promise me that if you feel light-headed or sick at all, you'll call an ambulance right away."

That I could agree to. "I promise."

Chief McTavish helped fast-track my discharge. The doctor insisted on listing it as *against medical advisement* even though he said I should be fine. I couldn't blame him. He had to cover his hind end in case I collapsed.

When we reached the police station, Chief McTavish led me past the front desk and to a metal door with the world's tiniest window. It couldn't be terribly useful unless you wanted to peek inside to make sure your suspect was where you'd left them before you entered, but its original intention was no doubt lost in the past. The Fair Haven police station didn't look like it'd been updated in decades.

The chief had his hand on the doorknob.

I stretched an arm out in front of him and planted my hand on the doorframe, blocking his path. "I need a minute to confer with my client before we begin."

The expression that flickered across his face bore a passing resemblance to respect. Had he been testing me? Waiting to see if I'd want to hear her story so she could actually answer some of his questions rather than simply blocking his investigation entirely?

He backed away with a nod, and I entered the room alone.

Holly was perched on her chair, one ankle tucked beneath her other knee. They'd left her with her phone, and the squishing noises coming from it made me think she was playing one of those bug-squashing games. She'd pulled her hair up into a messy topknot and had put too much makeup under her eyes, probably to try to cover the purple there. She hadn't succeeded.

Holly glanced up and set her phone down on the table. "Finally. I've been here for like two hours."

I didn't need to glance at my watch to know it'd been half an hour at most. "Did they read you your rights and tell you why you're here?"

"Drew." His name came out hesitant and low, like she wanted to hold onto it. "They're blaming me for...for what happened."

The fact that she stumbled over saying that Drew was dead gave me hope that Nancy and Daisy were right about her.

My parents had a private rule. They insisted on honesty from their clients about their guilt. You defended an innocent person differently than you did a guilty one. Not better or worse, according to them, just differently. You had to be on your guard for different traps and different arguments. In my time working for them, they hadn't defended many innocent people. That meant I had less practice with it as well.

But the first step was always to forge a connection with your client so they trusted you. I rounded the table and selected the chair next to Holly. I angled it so I faced her rather than the table and settled in. She watched me closely.

"I'm on your side," I said, "and I'm here to protect you, but first I need you to tell me the truth. Did you kill him?"

Her lip did an honest-to-goodness quiver, and her mouth opened, but nothing came out. Instead, she slowly shook her head.

I held her gaze for a moment longer, waiting for a tell that she was lying to me. She didn't look away, and her body language stayed open. She didn't reach for her phone or elaborate. The simple head shake was it. And I believed her.

I dug a tissue out of my pocket and handed it to her. "I need you to walk me through what happened that day, especially how you ended up with Drew's blood on your gloves."

"I did what you told us and went out looking for the little girl, but..." Holly fingered the corner of her jeans' cuff. She looked up at me. "Do I have to tell everything? It's embarrassing."

I ran my hands over my thighs. People misunderstood each other every day. Body language, for all it could tell about a person, was even harder to read accurately. Holly's embarrassment was going to read as guilt to Chief McTavish. "You have to tell all of it, and try not to be embarrassed about it, okay? They've heard a lot worse than anything you'll have to say."

Holly bobbed her head. "I was afraid of getting lost and not being able to find my way back. I kept imagining everyone having to spread out to look for me. So I turned around early."

The pink that spread up into her cheeks made her look like a china doll. If this had to go to trial, her looks should play to her advantage. I gave her a keep-going nod.

"When I got back to the sleigh, Drew was on the ground and there was—" She pressed a hand over her mouth and her throat worked like she was trying not to gag.

It'd be justice in a way if she threw up on me. The thought alone triggered my gag reflex as well. I could just imagine Chief McTavish coming back to find us both bent over the trash can.

I swallowed hard and rubbed her upper arm. "You can do this."

She touched her fingertips to her temple in the same spot Drew'd been stabbed. "All I could think was I needed to stop the bleeding. If I could stop the bleeding, someone could save him. But then I realized he wasn't breathing."

Drew had likely died instantly, given the location and force of the blow. Nothing Holly could do would have helped him. "That's how you got blood on your gloves."

She nodded.

"But why run?" I motioned back toward the door Chief McTavish would come through when he joined us. "The police would have believed you if you hadn't run."

"Drew introduced me to everyone as his assistant. I thought whoever killed him would come after me next."

I felt the weight of her fear through my shoulders and down my back. She might not have been wrong. Assuming whoever killed Drew was also the person who broke into Drew and Holly's homes, the killer connected them enough to suspect Holly might be hiding something that could implicate them.

"Did Drew leave anything with you for safekeeping that could make you a target?"

She touched her pinky finger along the crack in her lip and shook her head. "But the police should have found the pictures he was taking. He told me he was going to break a big story that he hoped would get him noticed by newspapers from the bigger cities. He wanted to start building up a portfolio so he'd have an easier time getting a job once we graduated."

Now Holly might not even have a chance to go to college.

At least her story fit with what we'd already learned. The big story had to be Shawn White's drug activities. A high school teacher dealing to his students would have probably gotten picked up by the *Grand Rapids Press*.

Chief McTavish would be back any minute, and I had one more thing I had to cover with Holly before he did. He'd no doubt ask her about the fight she had with Drew. As long as her story matched with what Daisy and Amy said, and she didn't try to hold back on the details because she was embarrassed by her jealousy, we'd be okay.

"The police have a witness who remembers seeing you and Drew fighting shortly before his murder. You're going to need to be able to explain the fight. Your mom said it was because a friend suggested Drew might be cheating on you."

The blush I'd expected came, but it was different. Not pink and in her cheeks. Instead, her ears and neck went red. Her gaze shifted slightly, like she was looking at a point above my left temple. "Yeah, Amy Powers. But Drew was just trying to keep her out of trouble. He even made sure to arrange the tour we'd be on to match the one she and her dad were on so I could meet her and see there wasn't anything going on."

There was a new note in her voice, like the softness was forced instead of natural.

Crap, crap, and double crap. I rubbed a hand over my eyes. Everything she said matched with what she told her mom at the time and what Amy told me later, but every innate lie-detector fiber in my body said she wasn't telling me the whole story.

If she was withholding it from me, she'd probably withheld it from her mom, too. Amy would have only known her own side of it all, not what happened privately between Drew and Holly.

The problem was that I didn't know her well enough to know how to approach it. Did I try to act like her friend and weasel it out, or did I play hardball?

I checked my watch. Ten minutes had already passed. We didn't have time for nice. If she lied to the police like she'd just lied to me, they were going to charge her with Drew's murder, and they had enough circumstantial evidence that they had a good chance at getting a conviction.

I needed to know what she was hiding before Chief McTavish forced it out of her. I crossed my arms over my chest and waited for her to make eye contact. After I was silent a couple of seconds, she looked at me.

"I don't defend people who lie to me," I said. "I need the whole story."

Her expression said *you wouldn't dare.*

I made sure mine replied *try me.* I'd told Nancy I didn't defend people who were guilty, and right now, I wasn't convinced anymore that Holly hadn't killed Drew, regardless of how sincere she'd looked when she swore she hadn't.

She must have seen I was serious about walking out because her mouth drooped open. "You'd really drop me as a client."

I channeled my mom's iron mask. "The deal is I represent you so long as you don't lie to me. You lied to me."

"I didn't lie." She pouted her full lips. "I might not have told everything, but I didn't lie."

"What did you leave out?"

She slid her phone back and forth along the table. "Do we have to tell the police if I tell you?"

"Not necessarily. It depends on whether it'll help prove you're innocent or not."

Ug. That made me sound like my parents, but it was true. If she was innocent, I wasn't going to have her tell the police something that would make her seem guilty.

"I wasn't mad at Drew because he met with Amy. He told me he was going to do it before he went. I was mad because..." She pulled her bottom lip into her mouth and sucked on it for a second. "We'd been working and saving so hard, and he decided we should give some of what we'd saved for school to Amy and her dad because they were having trouble paying their medical bills. He thought she was going to do something stupid otherwise even after his warning."

He wasn't wrong. Amy was determined if nothing else. The same quality that probably earned her scholarship could have been the one that lost it for her.

"It wasn't fair." Holly's voice kicked up a notch in vulnerable anger. "She already had a scholarship. She was going to go to school. So what if they had to go without a few other things in the meantime? Amy had twice what Drew and I did growing up. I told Drew if he gave away our money, he and I were done."

The back of my throat burned. You don't have to like your clients, my dad used to say. It's not our job to be their friends.

It still would have made this a lot easier if Holly didn't have a way of shaving down my nerves like they'd been stuck in a pencil sharpener. It was hard not to judge her as selfish and shallow, but I also didn't know what it was like to grow up in her circumstances. I'd had everything I could want and more, including a free ride to not only college but law school as well.

Amy hadn't mentioned Drew offering her money, so it seemed like Drew might have caved. But if that were the case, why would Holly still be harboring so much anger? It felt like the way to get the most out of Holly was to avoid direct questions for the moment, and see what came out. The girl didn't have much of a filter. "You two seemed to have made up by the time of the tour."

Her shoulders curled in. "Drew came back to me a couple days later and said he'd figured out a way we could keep our school money but help Amy and her dad, too."

My chest felt like someone was playing the drums on it from the inside out. If there were a legal way for Drew to make more money, he surely would have done it before then. That left only illegal means.

The two that came to mind were switching sides and selling drugs for Shawn White or blackmailing him.

Chapter 19

If Drew had been working for Shawn White, Shawn wouldn't have had a reason to kill him, so the most likely circumstance seemed that he'd decided to sell the photographs to Shawn rather than turning them over to the police.

The note had tried to warn me that Drew was a bad person, and I hadn't wanted to hear it. Not that Shawn White was the good person the note claimed, but he thought he was doing the students a service. He saw himself as good, and the note-writer never claimed objectivity.

Though the handwriting hadn't matched Shawn or Kristen's, and none of this explained how Shawn could have managed to kill Drew given the circumstances.

I couldn't risk becoming so fixated on Shawn being responsible for Drew's murder that I missed other possible explanations. It still felt like none of the possible suspects could have done it.

"Did Drew tell you what he planned to do?" My voice came out about how I'd expect it to sound if a bouncer-sized man had his hands wrapped around my throat.

Holly gave me a funny look like she couldn't figure out why *I* would be upset.

She couldn't—she didn't know me—but since coming to Fair Haven, I'd always fought to solve the murders of people who'd died trying to do good. They'd been white hats, whereas Drew's attire was gray at best. The thought made me feel like I'd been wearing the same pair of dirty clothes for weeks.

And now I was stuck defending a person I didn't like for the murder of a person who might have brought it on himself.

"He didn't want me getting involved, so he wouldn't tell me the details."

The annoyance in her voice made me want to shake her. Drew had clearly been trying to protect her, and it'd been trying to keep her happy that had led him down this path to begin with. None of that, as my parents would say, was my business, though. My business was casting reasonable doubt on the assertion that my client had committed the murder.

"He did tell me that he saw something while spying on the person for his big story," Holly said. "He'd originally planned to turn the other info over to the police at the same time as he broke his story, but no one would get hurt if he didn't, so we could use it instead."

Foolish me had handed Drew's SD card over to the police without looking at every picture on it because I'd assumed—wrongly—that the murderer must be Shawn White. I'd wanted him to be the guilty one because he was a drug dealer preying on kids, and he'd tried to kill me.

I was going to have to figure out a way to convince Chief McTavish to allow me to see the images again.

A brief knock on the door preceded Chief McTavish entering the room.

My understanding of Holly's story turned out not to matter. As Chief McTavish interrogated her, she completely ignored my signals as if she didn't even see them, answered questions he'd never asked, and tangled up her response to his questions about her argument with Drew so that it sounded like she might have been willing to kill him. I made sure that she clarified that she and Drew reconciled, but it was too little, much too late.

By the time Chief McTavish was done, I didn't have to ask what would happen next. Holly had made herself look guilty enough that if he didn't arrest her, he could be accused of negligence at best and favoritism at worst.

As he led her from the room to take her to booking, Holly looked back over her shoulder at me like a child being taken from her mother at the hospital. I really was a newbie at being primary on a case. I hadn't remembered to tell her what would happen next.

I followed after them. "Wait. I need one more minute with her."

Holly wrapped both hands around my wrist, clinging. Her eyes were too wide for her face, and tears ran down her cheeks. "I want to go home."

The same feeling I'd had—the need to comfort and protect—with Drew's mom and Amy flooded through me. I could almost hear my mother's critique, that it was my biological clock and maternal instincts and that I should have a child of my own so I could retain objectivity in my work. I prayed that my paranoid projection of her opinion was wrong. I wanted a child someday, but I wanted motherhood to make me more compassionate to others, not less.

I placed my free hand over Holly's. "They're going to hold you until you're arraigned. It should happen tomorrow, before the weekend. The judge will set bail then, and I'll try to get you home, okay?"

She was shaking her head. "We can't afford bail."

Given that Holly had already proven herself a flight risk, bail would be high. She was right to be scared. As much as I might want to help financially, I couldn't, not unless I could also equip Holly with a tracker anklet and handcuff her to my radiator—if I'd had one.

Wise people didn't gamble their business and the livelihood of their employees on someone who'd already shown they would run if they got scared.

I couldn't say any of that. It'd only make her more afraid. "Don't worry about that right now. We'll figure it out."

Chief McTavish handed her off to a waiting officer.

I stood in the middle of the waiting area and watched until they disappeared through a door. It felt like all the air had been sucked from the room, leaving me in a vacuum that crushed my lungs.

I couldn't do this. Not solo. Not without some much better lawyer to put into words the arguments that I built. With so much evidence against Holly, I wasn't a skilled enough attorney to get her acquitted if this went to trial. Unless I could find enough solid evidence against someone else to have the charges against her dismissed, she was going to spend her maturing years in prison. And when she came out, the girl she was— both good and bad—would be gone forever. She might have been better off with a public defender. Whoever she got might not care about her or her case, but they'd at least be able to string two coherent sentences together in public.

World's smallest violin, I could almost hear my dad saying. Successful people don't waste time feeling sorry for themselves.

Sometimes I thought it was a wonder with parents like mine that I hadn't rebelled, joined a biker gang, and ended up pregnant at sixteen.

But he was partly right this once. I didn't have time to feel sorry for myself. I had twenty-four hours to prove that Holly didn't kill Drew. That meant I had to get those pictures from Chief McTavish today.

Chapter 20

Chief McTavish had retired to his office without so much as a goodbye. If I asked permission to see him, he might turn me away and tell me to come back later or to wait until after Holly's arraignment, so this seemed like one of those times it was better to ask forgiveness instead.

I pretended to be searching around in my purse for my phone in case the desk officer looked up, and I slowly worked my way back toward the chief's office.

I didn't knock.

Chief McTavish had a phone in one hand, a pen in the other, and a look on his face that said I must be a hallucination because I couldn't have possibly just done what I did.

In hindsight, this might have been unwise. An angry chief was a chief who would refuse my request. I was so tired, I knew I wasn't thinking straight. I'd deserve any lecture I got from Mark later about leaving the hospital. And he'd better get here soon to pick me up, since my judgment was clearly impaired.

The chief set the phone back in its cradle and stared at me.

I needed to say something good. Fast.

"I'm sorry to burst in on you like this, but you disappeared before I had a chance to ask for some of the material I need." That didn't really excuse barging into his office. "I'm still not feeling well, and I wasn't sure I would be alright if I had to wait."

I dropped into the nearest chair. It wasn't entirely a lie.

The chief didn't respond, but his face went back to nuanced pink instead of the flat red it was trending toward.

"I'm going to need a better look at the pictures on the SD card I turned in to you," I said. "They could be instrumental in defending Holly."

Another partial truth. If I told him that I was looking for another suspect in those photos, he might not give them to me. He might simply assign one of his officers to look through them, and I couldn't leave this in someone else's hands.

He straightened the picture frames on his desk. "I did my homework better after our last meeting."

That would explain his slightly less antagonistic behavior toward me recently. I almost asked him what, exactly, he'd found out, but that would have come across as needy, and I wasn't sure I wanted to know. My parents were the ones with the reputation for results, as well as for being cutthroat and agnostic to the guilt of their clients. I'd been known for not living up to their reputation and finally quitting because I couldn't hack it—the disappointing daughter of two success stories.

I clamped my lips shut and waited for Chief McTavish to continue on his own.

He scratched an eyebrow with his thumb and broke eye contact for two blinks. "I'm willing to admit when I'm wrong, and I hope we can have a good professional relationship. Ask for a copy of the pictures out front." He picked up the phone receiver again. "That doesn't mean I have to like you. You still poke your nose in where it doesn't belong." He pointed the receiver at the door. "Now get out of my office."

The desk officer gave me a disk of the photos that were on the SD card at almost the same moment Mark walked through the front doors.

Mark waited until we were alone in my car to ask about it.

I filled him in on what I'd learned from Holly. I'd gotten her permission to share the information with whoever I needed in order to put together a strong defense. "Since she said he spotted whatever it was while surveilling Shawn White's drug trade, it should be in among the other pictures he took."

"Theoretically, but we don't know what we're looking for."

True enough. I redirected my gaze out the window. The sky was a light blue, leaning toward purple as the sun set, but the roads were still darker than usual and full of puddles, suggesting it'd rained earlier in the day. Russ had told me that with the start of the spring rains, the tourist season was officially over. If I had any takers for my free replacement tour, I'd be driving them out in our wagon rather than the sleigh and hoping we didn't get bogged down in the mud. The snow that had covered the ground a few days ago had disappeared completely.

I wasn't going out into the woods with any of them, though, until we were sure which one had killed Drew. My involvement in the case wasn't a secret any longer, and I wasn't stupid enough to knowingly put myself in a dangerous situation. Despite what Mark might think, I didn't want to die.

I looked back at Mark's profile. One of the nice perks of our relationship that I hadn't thought about before we started dating was that I could watch him without it being weird. "I was thinking that maybe he'd gotten shots of whatever group has been robbing the houses. If we could figure out from the pictures where they were taken, then we can see if any break-ins were reported in that area. We should be able to get the time and date from the metadata if we see anything unusual in the photos to corroborate."

"Erik said a couple of the kids they identified from the photos already also confessed to robbing houses to get money for the drugs. The chief basically advocated for leniency for them as long as they completed their community service and worked to pay back what they'd taken. If all we see in Drew's pictures is them coming out of a house that doesn't belong to them, I don't think they're responsible for Drew's murder. None of them were on the tour."

I gouged a nail into the seam in my car door. Another theory foiled. On top of Mark's very logical conclusion, if it'd been teenagers committing the break-ins, Drew probably wouldn't have tried to blackmail them anyway.

At this rate, Holly was going to jail, and it'd break both Nancy and Daisy's hearts. "Do you mind helping me look anyway?"

"Have I said no to you yet? Besides, you should still be under medical supervision. A few more nights and I won't even notice the lumps in your couch anymore."

Chapter 21

We arrived back to my house to the aroma of lasagna baking in the oven.

My mouth watered. After hospital food, my cooking would have tasted like a gourmet feast, and this smelled a million times better. Except I knew Mark's culinary skills weren't any better than mine. He'd either bought it or... "Please tell me your mom didn't make us a lasagna."

Mark gave me a sheepish grin. "She was already making a pan for them, so she said it was no trouble."

There was no redeeming this. Not only had I thrown up on her, probably ruining whatever she'd been wearing, but she now knew I couldn't cook. "How are you going to survive my cooking long-term with a mom who can bake lasagna that smells like that?"

His gaze dipped to my lips, and his grin turned cheeky. "You have other redeeming qualities."

His lips barely had time to brush mine before the soft squeaking from the laundry room where the dogs were turned into full-blown howling. They wanted out to see me. Immediately.

Mark pulled away and headed for the door. "Toby's been okay, but I couldn't even get Velma interested in her toys. She's been lying by the door, waiting for you to come home."

Two cone-heads emerged from the room as soon as Mark released them from their crates.

Worry spiked in my chest. "What happened to To-by?"

Velma, with her experience wearing the cone, stopped in time, but Toby rammed into my leg, hard, and nearly knocked me over. I grabbed the edge of the kitchen counter to stay upright.

Mark wisely stayed outside of the bruise zone of cones and tails. "He's fine. I didn't want to worry you while you were in the hospital and couldn't do anything about it, but I had to take Velma back to the vet because her incision started to ooze."

"How should that not worry me?" I tried to get a better look at Toby, but he wouldn't stop moving, and Velma kept pushing him aside. I wasn't going to be able to get a decent look at either of them while they were circling me like piranhas that fed on cuddles. "Now I have two sick dogs."

"One sick dog. One dog who can't keep his tongue to himself."

Wait, what? I stopped trying to examine them and let them continue wriggling around me. "You're telling me Toby is wearing a cone because he's the one who's been causing Velma problems with her incision?"

Mark nodded. "The vet figures Toby thought he was helping her by cleaning a wound she couldn't take care of herself."

I made a *bleck* face. "I'm honestly not sure whether to find that adorable or disgusting."

At least that was one mystery solved. The vet had said Velma shouldn't have been able to reach the incision, and the allergy treatments weren't working. We'd hit a dead end. Not unlike Drew's case.

Mark was saying something to me, but a ringing sound had filled my ears. What if we'd done the same thing in Drew's case? I'd believed the real killer had to be a reasonably tall man because of the angle of the blow. Mark assumed the same thing. That's not what the evidence told us, though. It said whoever struck Drew was at a certain angle. One that might have been created by Drew squatting down and the killer standing up.

That meant the killer could have been a woman. Or a short man.

Mark waved a hand in front of my face like we were in a nineties sitcom. "Did the doctor check you for a concussion?"

I batted his hand away. "My head's fine. I think I found a flaw in our theory about who could have killed Drew the way he died."

I explained it to Mark.

"You're right," he said.

The oven timer went, and he slid on my purple-checkered oven mitts.

Heat spiraled down into my belly. Those goofy mitts and the way he took care of me and my dogs made him extra sexy. The physical boundaries Mark and I had decided to put on our relationship were new territory for me, and at times like this, it was hard to remember why we thought they were important. It was also hard to focus on anything but him.

"But right now that's your one trump card for defending Holly," Mark said.

That hard truth snapped me back to what I should be paying attention to—that I might have single-handedly destroyed Holly's one hope at freedom.

Sometimes I hated how often Mark was right. Nancy would never forgive me if I accidentally proved Holly had done it. "I did tell them I wouldn't defend Holly if she turned out to be guilty. I'd insist she take a plea deal or find another lawyer."

Mark set the lasagna on top of the oven to cool for a few minutes. "Have you changed your mind about Holly's innocence?"

All the evidence pointed to her, but I'd watched her lie to me, and I'd seen the difference in her when she told the truth. I'd also seen how flustered she got when trying to tell her story. Unless she'd faked all her reactions to throw us off—and she'd have to be a high-functioning sociopath to be able to succeed at that—she'd been telling the truth when she said she didn't kill Drew.

On top of that, Nancy had so much faith in Holly. Love blinded people, but Nancy told me on her visit before my poisoning that Daisy was exactly like Holly at her age, and Daisy turned out well. Holly deserved that chance, too.

"I need to be able to prove that Drew wasn't standing up before it would even matter."

The killer could have forced Drew to his knees, but that would have required a weapon, and if they'd had a threatening weapon, they would have killed him with it rather than with my maple syrup tap.

I closed my eyes and tried to picture where I'd found Drew. He'd been lying in the snow at the base of one of the display trees with his camera next to him, so he'd likely been taking pictures right before he was attacked. I knew firsthand that Drew had a knack for finding unique angles. "He might have been kneeling or squatting to get the perfect camera angle."

I grabbed my phone before Mark could talk me out of it and dialed Erik's number. I put it on speaker so Mark could hear as well.

Erik answered on the first ring. That was good. He was probably at the station and could check what I wanted.

"Before you tell me that you can't tell me anything, Chief McTavish has given me some access to the information around Drew's case because I'm Holly Northgate's lawyer."

"Most people start with hello, Nicole." His voice had that tone that said he was smiling on the inside even if his lips weren't showing it. "Leading with that makes me think I'll have to say *no* to what you're gonna ask, but you can ask anyway."

I wouldn't put it past Erik to shut me down if he thought it would violate the rules. Maybe I should have called Elise instead, but she'd been taken off the case, and asking her to look up anything was like throwing her to the lions—or, more specifically, the lion. "All I want to know is the angle of the last photo Drew Harris took."

The squeak of his chair and the mumble of voices too far away to be heard clearly filled the line.

"Okay," Erik said, "that's strange, but since the chief gave you other photos in the case, I can't see a reason he would object to that."

I couldn't hear if he was clicking computer keys, but I imagined the sounds anyway.

"It's a picture of trees and a wooden bucket," he finally said.

That explained why the police hadn't put this together before either. They'd only looked at the pictures to see if Drew took a picture of a person prior to his death. When they saw nothing other than my trees and a maple syrup collection display, they'd moved on. "Where is it taken from? Straight on? From above?"

"Looks like he might have been kneeling, looking up at it. Now are you going to tell me what this is about?"

"I'll call you back when I know."

I caught the front end of a sigh as I disconnected, but I wasn't going to give away what I'd figured out yet. That would have felt like betraying my duty to Holly. Besides, Erik was a good officer. He's probably run with what I'd had him look at and put it together himself.

I had to hope I hadn't burned my bridge while I was still standing on it. If we couldn't find evidence that would tell us who Drew meant to blackmail, the final hole that sunk Holly might have been drilled by me.

As soon as we finished a very generous helping of Mrs. Cavanaugh's lasagna, along with a salad to make it feel a little healthier, we settled in together on the couch with my laptop and the disc of Drew's pictures.

My eyes wanted to drift shut. All I wanted was to tuck in close to Mark and rest my head on his shoulder. I hadn't fully realized how much the poisoning had weakened me until I'd tried to go through a normal day.

But I couldn't. Holly would be arraigned sometime tomorrow. All I had was tonight to figure out how to get the charges dropped.

I checked the date on the first image and the date on the last one. They'd been taken over a two-week span, with the final set taken the day before Drew confronted Amy. He must have stopped taking photos when he recognized her at the drop location. A quick skim showed that they were all taken at roughly the same spot, from different angles and at different times of day.

I moved the laptop a little more in Mark's direction. Sitting with him like this reminded me of the first case we'd worked together, trying to figure out who'd killed my Uncle Stan. "Do you recognize the location?"

He zoomed one of the photos in slightly, then clicked to the next one and did the same. "I think it's the empty lot next to the animal shelter." He pointed to a building at the edge of the photo with wire fencing. "Doesn't that look like the dog runs?"

He was right. Fortunately or unfortunately, that was on the edge of town, and there weren't any homes close enough to it that Drew could have caught a glimpse of the teenage thieves. None of the businesses in that area had been broken into. That, surely, would have made the rounds of the rumor mill. Not even Chief McTavish would have been able to keep it quiet.

We flipped our way through all the pictures. Nothing jumped out as an ideal blackmail opportunity. I'd kind of hoped we'd find a picture of someone who wasn't on our tour mugging an old granny or hiring a prostitute, but it was all pictures of Shawn with his clients or vehicles. Some of my desire to go to sleep rather than face these photos probably came from wanting everyone in my tour group to be innocent.

We had to be looking for something connected to a member of the tour group. Drew could have been blackmailing any of the people buying from Shawn, but Holly said it'd been something *else* he'd seen. None of the buyers were on the tour except Amy, whose pictures were noticeably absent. Drew had probably deleted them. He definitely hadn't been thinking of blackmailing her since the blackmail money was for her and her dad.

It was possible Holly had been wrong or that the pictures Drew told her about were on a different memory card seized by the police or on the computer taken by the thief. The latter seemed the least likely. Drew wouldn't have put something like that on the desktop his whole family had access to. But even the former didn't make sense. The police would have noticed pictures that looked out of place.

"Did Erik say anything about strange pictures on what they took from Drew's house?" I asked.

"Nope. All of them were from legit jobs Drew'd been hired for, mostly small stuff like family photos."

We had to narrow our search down. "Let's focus on only the photos that don't show Shawn."

Mark skimmed through them again. Drew had taken a couple close-ups of Shawn's license plate—what little could be seen of the rest of the car matched Shawn's vehicle—probably as additional proof that it was him.

Two other Shawn-less images showed another car, stopped in the middle of the street with a person in front of it. The lighting was so low that it was impossible to make out details beyond that the person in front of it looked like a man and the person in the driver's seat looked like a woman.

The car was a lipstick-red four-door SUV. I didn't know enough about cars to name the manufacturer or model, but it was one of those that I hated the appearance of because they reminded me of a hearse. You didn't see many of them in Fair Haven, but I'd seen one.

In the parking lot of The Sunburnt Arms, with an Ohio license plate.

Chapter 22

I must have turned gray because Mark pressed a hand to my forehead, like concern for me made him forget he couldn't accurately check for a fever that way.

I pulled his hand off my forehead and held it clasped in both of mine. "I'm fine."

But I wasn't. I just didn't know yet how to explain all the emotions surging through me.

The Marshalls were supposed to be here on a second honeymoon. Their chance to make up for all the past mistakes. Their chance to find happiness. Not so different from Mark and me, both of us finding a second chance at happiness in each other after the tragedies we'd been through.

If the Marshalls turned out to be the ones who'd killed Drew, it'd be over when it'd barely had time to start.

This case didn't have a happy ending. It had endings where we caught the true killer and the innocent people went free, but no matter who went to prison for Drew's murder, it'd leave carnage behind. Nancy and the Northgates losing a girl who, for all her selfish, silly ways brought joy into their lives. Shawn White's children growing up without their dad. Amy separated from her dad. Or the Marshalls spending what should have been their love-filled retirement years in prison.

The least-damaging scenario was that Shawn had killed Drew because he was going to prison for his crimes anyway, but try as I might, I couldn't find a way to finagle him into the role of Drew's killer.

My hand shook so much that I practically poked my screen, trying to point to the car. "Zoom in. That car belongs to the Marshalls."

Mark squinted at the screen. "How can you be sure?" He zoomed in on the driver. "Even close up the faces are too shadowy to see, and you can't see the license plate from this angle."

Neither of those were what I needed to see. I put my own hand on the trackpad and moved the center of the enlarged image toward the back window of the car. There it was. "I'm sure. Their car has the same decal in the same place."

"It's the Cincinnati Bengals," Mark said. "Is that where they're from?"

I nodded.

"Even if we can figure out why this picture would motivate murder, I thought you'd already ruled the Marshalls out," Mark said. "The handwriting didn't match."

The shock was wearing off, and the pieces were trying to fall together in my brain almost faster than I could catch them.

"I checked his handwriting, but not hers, because we were assuming it was a man. Even the fact that the note was handwritten fits. Mandy doesn't have an office center with a printer for her guests, and they couldn't very well ask her to print the note off for them. She would have read it. If we can figure out the why behind this, Chief McTavish can bring them back in for questioning and ask for a handwriting sample. They had to be in this together." I rubbed at my ribs more out of habit than pain. "When was the picture taken?"

Mark right-clicked on the image and opened the box that showed all the information the image was automatically tagged with, including the date and time. It'd been taken less than a week before Drew's murder, but before his conversation with Amy. Based on what I knew of when the Marshalls came to town, the picture was likely taken the evening they arrived. That could be easily checked with Mandy if necessary.

I was probably a fool, but I was still hoping it wasn't necessary.

I enlarged the image again, but it turned grainy. I'd zoomed in too far. I backed it out again.

A thin bit of silver by the man in front of the car caught my eye. A black, ball-shaped object lay on the ground beside it.

Dear God, it couldn't be. It looked like a small part of a person and bicycle handlebars. Like they'd hit someone. "Do you remember what day that boy was injured by the hit-and-run driver a couple weeks ago?"

Mark gave me a where-did-that-come-from look. I touched my finger to the screen beside where he should look. It wasn't obvious. If we hadn't been zoomed in so closely, I might not have noticed it.

"I'm not sure," Mark said. "He didn't end up on my slab, but there was an article about it in the paper."

He typed the address of the Fair Haven Weekly into my Internet browser and clicked back two issues. Since that week's issue came out before Drew's murder, the hit-and-run accident made the featured story.

Not only did the date match the one on Drew's photo, but the estimated time fit with the time on the picture.

Mark slumped back into the couch and ran a hand through his hair. "I don't understand. If they'd called it in, they'd have been fine. The kid admitted to riding out into the street from the alleyway without looking.

Now they're facing jail time for this, even aside from Drew's murder."

Mr. Marshall's words came back to me as if he stood in the room. I'm not going to let anything take her away from me again.

I moved the photo around to show the driver again.

The driver was a woman. Mrs. Marshall wasn't allowed to drive. The doctor pulled her license because of her seizures. My throat spasmed shut. They couldn't call the police and tell the truth. If they'd been thinking clearly, they might have been able to pretend Ted Marshall had been driving instead of Janet, but no one's thinking clearly right after hitting someone with their car. I could vouch for that personally.

I closed my laptop lid. I couldn't stand to look at it anymore.

Something else was also niggling at the back of my mind. Something Mr. Marshall said about a change in their plans. "What day is it?"

"Thursday. Why?"

"The Marshalls are about to leave the country."

Chapter 23

Mark dialed Chief McTavish for the second time. He wasn't answering. He left a message and dialed again.

"What time is check-out at The Sunburnt Arms?" he asked while listening to the call ring.

"Eleven. If they planned to fly out of the Grand Rapids airport..."

"...they could be gone already," Mark finished for me.

I typed *non-extradition countries USA* into my search bar and read the results. If they traveled to a non-extradition country, there'd be nothing anyone could do to bring them back to stand trial for Drew's murder. "Crap. The Maldives don't have an extradition treaty with the U.S."

Mark tapped the cancel-call icon on his phone. "I'll try Erik." He dialed with his thumb. "Would they really leave everything behind? I'm assuming they have a house? Family?"

They might have both those things, but Ted Marshall had made it clear where his priorities lay when I spoke with him shortly after Drew's murder. He couldn't let anything happen to Janet, and he couldn't stand to lose her. If staying together meant leaving everything, I didn't doubt he'd do it. "Family could visit them. The rest is only stuff."

Mark held up his pointer finger and said something into his phone. He must have gotten through to Erik.

In my Internet search bar, I typed *flights from Gerald R Ford Intl to Maldives*. Each result said the same thing—no non-stop flights. I clicked through to one of the links that listed the actual possible flight times and routes. Bingo. "Tell Erik all the flights from Grand Rapids have a layover in Chicago. They might still be able to contact the authorities there and catch them if they're on the plane already."

I woke up hours later with a kink in my neck, the movie Mark and I decided to watch since I didn't think I'd be able to sleep playing on the TV, and Mark reaching across me.

He snagged his phone from the end table and answered it. "Hang on," he said. "I'll put you on speaker. Nikki will want to hear this too."

He turned the TV off, tapped the phone's screen, and rested the phone on his knee.

"I'll be a gentleman and not ask what you're doing at Nicole's house at two in the morning," Erik's voice said from the phone.

"He's sleeping *on my couch* until I'm well enough to be on my own." I massaged the side of my neck, but the knot wouldn't let go. Though if Erik was right about the time, it was no wonder. "Did you catch them?"

"Not personally, but the Chicago PD has them in custody."

I didn't know whether to roll my eyes at his precision or let loose a Velma-esque happy wiggle that they hadn't escaped.

"They faxed us a handwriting sample from Janet Marshall, and it matched," Erik continued. "And we were able to get their car from where they abandoned it at the airport. There's only a small ding in the front fender, but that's consistent with the hit-and-run with the biker. Whoever hit him barely clipped his front tire, so we didn't expect the vehicle to show much damage. Along with the pictures from Drew Harris and the handwriting match, though, it was enough. Janet Marshall confessed to hitting the kid, and Ted Marshall confessed to murdering Drew."

I hadn't expected them to cave so easily, but they weren't hardened criminals. That's part of what was so upsetting about it all. They were normal people who made some very bad choices—like allowing Janet to drive when she shouldn't have. "Did they say how the hit-and-run happened?"

"Yeah. Ted Marshall got tired on the drive up here and started to fall asleep at the wheel. Since they were so close and there wasn't really anywhere they could stop to sleep until they reached Fair Haven, his wife offered to drive. They thought it wouldn't matter that she didn't have a license for a short stretch, and it'd be safer than Ted continuing on. When the kid rode right out in front of her and got hit, they panicked. The fall knocked the kid unconscious, but he was still breathing, so they figured he'd be okay and it wouldn't hurt anyone for them to just leave."

Mark took over massaging my neck for me. His touch made concentrating on what Erik was saying difficult, but I didn't want him to stop. He was succeeding at working out the tense muscle where I'd failed.

"Except that Drew saw it happen," Mark said.

"And tried to blackmail them for it," I added.

Erik grunted an agreement. "Drew told them to take the tour that day and bring the money. Our best guess is he thought they must have a lot of money because they were tourists. He asked for an amount the Marshalls had no way of paying. They weren't struggling anywhere like the Powerses or Drew and Holly's families, but Janet's medical expenses meant they didn't have money to throw around, either."

I squeezed my eyes shut. It felt like a bad joke. Drew had tried to extort money from the Marshalls to help with George Powers' medical bills, but the Marshalls couldn't pay him off because of Janet's medical bills.

That's the part of it all that still didn't make sense to me. "Did they tell Drew why they couldn't pay? Surely he wouldn't have still insisted on the payoff once he knew."

"They did, and he didn't." Erik sucked in a breath and let it out slowly. "But he made the mistake of telling them he'd have to take what he knew to the police instead."

The rest was easy enough to figure out. "I'm surprised the Marshalls stayed in town afterward. I would have thought they'd leave right away rather than sticking around."

"I wondered about that, too," Erik said, "so I asked the Chicago PD to question them about it. Turns out they stayed after the hit-and-run because they wanted to be sure the kid was okay. Then after they killed Drew, they thought it'd be too suspicious if they left right away. When you didn't believe Holly had done it and started asking questions, they decided to send you that note to try to stop you, and they booked plane tickets as a back-up plan. They didn't want to leave behind their life here if they didn't have to."

Mark stopped rubbing my neck, and I leaned into him. As much as I loved Mark, I couldn't fathom allowing someone else to go to prison for something he'd done. It wasn't right.

My lawyer's mind finally woke up enough to kick in. "All charges against Holly should be dropped, and she should be released."

"Chief McTavish is already working on it. She'll be out first thing in the morning."

Chapter 24

The next morning, Nancy picked me up in her car and brought me along with her so I could be there when Holly was officially released.

Holly practically threw herself at her parents, and the hugging spilled over to Nancy and myself.

"I'm taking them all out to brunch to celebrate," Nancy said to me when Holly let me go. "You're more than welcome to join us. We have Holly back, thanks to you."

I glanced sidelong at where Holly and Daisy stood wrapped in each other's arms again. "I appreciate it, but I think this should be a family—" I almost said celebration, but that didn't seem right given that there'd be a lot of grieving Holly and her parents still needed to do over Drew in the coming days and months. "Family event. If you could drop me off at Cavanaugh Funeral Home on your way, I'd appreciate it."

Because the county had a small budget for their police departments, Mark's office as medical examiner was an office at his family's funeral home that the county rented. Now that Holly was free, I couldn't put off meeting his parents and apologizing to his mom for the whole I-threw-up-on-you incident. The longer I waited, the more time my nerves would have to turn me into a neurotic woman who was sure to embarrass herself even more...assuming that was possible. I was hoping Mark would call them and ask them to go out to dinner with us tonight. That would give me time to prepare, and I should be able to show up looking presentable and without poison in my system.

Nancy agreed to drop me off, and the Northgates thanked me one more time.

"Could you guys pull up the cars?" Holly asked when they finished. "I want to talk to Nicole by myself."

The grown-ups left, and Holly turned her cell phone over and back again in her hands. "I need to ask your advice about something. You won't tell my parents I asked, right? It's still under the lawyer-client confidentiality thingy?"

My stomach twisted. Surely she couldn't have committed a different crime. This was starting to feel like the case that wouldn't end. "You're an adult. Whatever you tell me stays between us."

She glanced out the doorway as if making sure her parents weren't coming up behind her. "Drew didn't have a will or anything like that, but his mom wants me to take the money he'd been saving and use it for school. With what he'd saved so far, I'd be able to pay for my first couple years at least, and I could work during that time to pay for the rest."

Geez, she really shouldn't scare someone who'd been released from the hospital early that way. My poor poisoned heart couldn't take it. "That sounds like a good thing."

She chewed the corner of her bottom lip and shook her head rapidly. "I'm not stupid, and I had a lot of time to think last night. Drew wouldn't be dead"—she shoved the word out like it wouldn't have come unless she forced it—"if I hadn't been so mad about the whole Amy thing. I shouldn't get that money. Mrs. Harris should keep it, or she should give it to Amy and her dad."

Warmth filled my chest. That showed more maturity than I would have expected from Holly. I could see now what Nancy meant when she said Holly was more than she seemed and that she just needed some time to grow up. Drew must have seen it, too, and that's why he loved her so much.

"Drew's mom will be happier to see you go to school than she would be to have the money. I've talked to her a little bit, and what she wants most is to know that Drew's life counted for something. If you went to school and graduated and lived a full life, she could take joy in it because she'd feel like Drew made something good possible."

Holly gave one of those slow I'm-not-sure-I'm-convinced nods.

She wasn't going to be able to take the money and also overcome the guilt inside. "Could you give some of the money to the Powerses and still have enough to pay for at least your first year?"

Her nod gained confidence. "I think that would make Drew happy."

I ushered her toward the door before she could second-guess herself. "I think so, too."

She threw another hug at me, and we met her family outside. Nancy dropped me off as requested.

Grant didn't come out to greet me when I entered Cavanaugh Funeral Home. He was probably meeting with a bereaved family. I was familiar enough with where Mark's office was anyway that I didn't really need an escort. It's not like I'd go poking around in their freezer anyway. Shudder.

Two male voices drifted out through Mark's office door. I'd recognize the tone of Mark's voice anywhere. The other one had a similar timber—probably Grant.

I knocked while opening the door. If they were talking dead-body business, that would give them enough warning to stop.

The door hit something solid, and a woman screeched. I let go of the doorknob, but my feet refused to move. The screech sounded much too much like...

The door opened, and Mrs. Cavanaugh stood inside, one hand covering her nose. Grant sat on one corner of Mark's desk, his mouth gaping open. Mark perched on the other side. He looked a bit like he might be choking. Or trying not to laugh. I wasn't entirely sure which. It might have been a little of both.

If there was any justice in the world, a hole would have opened up in the floor and swallowed me. That it didn't was yet another proof that life wasn't fair.

"There are easier ways to keep from having to spend time with your boyfriend's mother, sweetie, I promise." Mrs. Cavanaugh rubbed her nose, but a half smile that looked eerily similar to her son's twisted her lips. "I tried enough of them in my younger days that I should know."

The heat that flamed into my cheeks could have roasted marshmallows. Mark was definitely laughing now.

If I became a permanent part of the Cavanaugh family one day, I was never, ever going to live this down.

Hot Mess Butter Tarts

INGREDIENTS:

16-18 unbaked tart shells (depending on the size of the shell)
1 cup raisins
3/4 cup brown sugar
1/4 cup softened butter
2 eggs
1/2 cup maple sugar
1 tablespoon flour
1 tablespoon vanilla extract
1 pinch salt

INSTRUCTIONS:

1. Preheat the oven to 350 degrees F (175 degrees C).

2. Set the frozen tart shells on a large baking sheet.

3. Add raisins to the tart shells.

4. In a medium-sized bowl, beat together the brown sugar and butter with an electric mixer until smooth.

5. Whisk in all the remaining ingredients.

6. Fill the tart shells about 3/4 of the way. (They puff up when you cook them, and if you fill them more than that, they'll bubble over.)

7. Bake until the tart shells are golden brown and the filling sets, about 15-20 minutes. If your oven doesn't cook evenly, turn the baking sheet halfway through to help with even baking.

8. Cool and eat.

MAKES 16-18 tarts.

LETTER FROM THE AUTHOR

I hope you enjoyed solving this mystery alongside Nicole, watching Nicole and Mark start to work out their relationship, and seeing more of her dogs. In the next book, Nicole's mom comes for a visit.

If you'd like to know as soon Book 5 (*Deadly Arms*) releases, sign up for my newsletter at www.smarturl.it/emilyjames.

If you enjoyed *Murder on Tap*, I'd really appreciate it if you also took a minute to write a quick review wherever you bought the book. Reviews help me sell more books (which allows me to keep writing them), and they also help fellow readers know if this is a book they might enjoy.

Love,
Emily

ABOUT THE AUTHOR

Emily James grew up watching TV shows like *Matlock*, *Monk*, and *Murder She Wrote*. (It's pure coincidence that they all begin with an M.) It was no surprise to anyone when she turned into a mystery writer.

She loves cats, dogs, and coffee. Lots and lots of coffee...lots and lots of cats, too. Seriously, there's hardly room in the bed for her husband. While they only have one dog, she's a Great Dane, so she should count as at least two.

If you'd like to know as soon as Emily's next mystery releases, please join her newsletter list at www.smarturl.it/emilyjames.

She also loves hearing from readers. You can email her through her website (www.authoremilyjames.com) or find her on Facebook (www.facebook.com/authoremilyjames/).

57315149R00153

Made in the USA
San Bernardino, CA
19 November 2017